BY THE WATERS OF MANHATTAN

BOOKS BY CHARLES REZNIKOFF

POETRY AND VERSE DRAMA

Rhythms (1918)
Rhythms II (1919)
Poems (1920)
Uriel Acosta: A Play & A Fourth Group of Verse (1921)
Chatterton, The Black Death & Meriwether Lewis,
       three plays (1922)
Coral & Captive Israel, two plays (1923)
Five Groups of Verse (1927)
Nine Plays (1927)
Jerusalem the Golden (1934)
In Memoriam: 1933 (1934)
Separate Way (1936)
Going To and Fro and Walking Up and Down (1941)
Inscriptions: 1944–1956 (1959)
By the Waters of Manhattan: Selected Verse (1962)
Testimony: The United States 1885–1890: Recitative (1965)
Testimony: The United States 1891–1900: Recitative (1968)
By the Well of Living and Seeing & The Fifth Book of
      the Maccabees (1969)
By the Well of Living and Seeing: New and Selected Poems
      1918–1973 (1974)
Holocaust (1975)
Poems 1918–1936: Volume 1 of The Complete Poems of
      Charles Reznikoff (1976)
Poems 1937–1975: Volume 2 of The Complete Poems of
      Charles Reznikoff (1977)
Poems 1918–1975: The Complete Poems of Charles Reznikoff
      (1989)
The Poems of Charles Reznikoff 1918–1975 (2005)

CHARLES REZNIKOFF

BY THE
WATERS
OF MANHATTAN

INTRODUCTION BY PHILLIP LOPATE

A BLACK SPARROW BOOK
DAVID R. GODINE · *Publisher · Boston*

This is a Black Sparrow Book
published in 2009 by
David R. Godine · Publisher
Post Office Box 450
Jaffrey, New Hampshire 03452
WWW.BLACKSPARROWBOOKS.COM

Copyright © 1930 by Charles Boni, Jr.
Reprinted by arrangement with David Bodansky
Introduction copyright © 2009 by Phillip Lopate

LIBRARY OF CONGRESS CATALOGING-IN-PUBLICATION DATA

Reznikoff, Charles, 1894-1976.
By the waters of Manhattan / introduction by Philip Lopate ; by
Charles Reznikoff. -- 1st Black Sparrow Books ed.
p. cm.
"A Black Sparrow book."
ISBN 978-1-57423-214-1
1. Jews—New York (State)—New York—Fiction. 2. Manhattan
(New York, N.Y.)—Fiction. 3. Jewish fiction. 4. Immigrants—Fiction.
5. Poets—Fiction. 6. Domestic fiction. I. Title.
PS3535.E98B8 2009
813'.52—dc22
2009003263

SECOND PRINTING, 2018
Printed in The United States

CONTENTS

THE RESILIENT ART OF CHARLES REZNIKOFF, OR, THE STYLE OF 'NO STYLE'

by Phillip Lopate

AMONG THOSE who cherish his tender, translucent, humane poetry, Charles Reznikoff is a venerated figure, a role model of integrity and sustained excellence. During most of his lifetime (1894–1976), he had been so underrated and neglected that he developed a kind of stoical, resigned shell, going his own way. In person (I saw him on numerous occasions before he died), Reznikoff gave off an obliging, almost meekly humble impression, but there was a stubborn will underneath; his dedication to his art was unshakeable. You can see it from his correspondence, that remarkable, moving record in *Selected Letters of Charles Reznikoff, 1917–1976* (Black Sparrow Press, 1997). If publishers would not accept his poetry manuscripts, he would print them himself. He also had that grain of selfishness that all writers need, however annoying to their loved ones. Though his wife Marie yearned for years to quit her high school teaching job, Charles, the most devoted, uxorious of husbands, nevertheless would not become a go-getter. He refused to practice law, though he had a degree. Instead, he held down jobs that would afford him the mental freedom to pursue poetry and fiction: he wrote tedious legal definitions for textbooks, sold hats, and, temperamentally ill-suited as he was to service the Hollywood dream factory, polished screenplays for his boyhood friend, producer Albert Lewin.

Towards the end of his life, he was taken up by the younger members of the New York School of poetry and the descendents of the Objectivists, and treated reverently by them, like a fragile, priceless grandparent, a last link to the pioneers of the twenties and thirties. Reznikoff, glad for the appreciation, did not know quite what to make of it, just as he had been puzzled decades earlier when championed by Louis Zukofsky (whose abstruse criticism he could barely decipher) as a sort of instinctual Objectivist poet. The problem with that annexation was that Reznikoff was no primitive: he was extremely intelligent, rigorous, and, in his own non-showy way, committed to an ambitiously austere aesthetic program of his own.

Thematically, his work showed a lively, unsentimental sympathy for those underdogs in the urban sweepstakes: the laborer, the beggar, the immigrant, the storeowner trying to eke out a living. Stylistically, he hewed to the diction of ordinary American speech, carving his material into tight, haiku-like images and wry vignettes that could best convey the often comical sufferings, struggles, contradictions, and consolations of the everyday human beings he observed, including himself. He also went to sources such as legal documents (for his long two-part prose poem *Testimony*), historical records (for the book-length poem *Holocaust*) and Biblical stories (*King David*) for his often unsparing, sometimes gruesomely realistic, verses.

His poetry, immensely appealing as it is, lacks only one quality that so far has kept it from being fully embraced by the academic literary establishment: "difficulty." There is nothing remotely arcane about it that would require professional interpretation; it speaks for itself ... or so it would at first appear. I would argue, however, that Reznikoff's work is very sophisticated and requires a good deal of unpacking, precisely because it seems so simple and straightforward. If true for the poetry, then even more so for the fiction.

Reznikoff wrote two novels: the first, the one you have in your hand, was published in 1930, just as the Great Depression was getting under way. One associates this writer with the Depression, partly because of the grey air of diminished expectations and pinched circumstances that seem to unify his characters, though their chronic money troubles had predated the 1929 stock market crash and would outlive the postwar boom years. Actually, 1930 was a highpoint for Reznikoff: he had won the hand of the lovely Marie Syrkin and convinced her to divorce her second husband, and he had finished his first novel, which the respected firm of Charles Boni agreed to publish.

(His second novel, *The Manner "Music"*, was found in his desk after he died and published posthumously in 1977. It is very bleak, set in the Depression years as well, and full of fine cutaway descriptions of the city, as two old friends engage in marathon walks, conversing about their dashed dreams and the bitterness of married life, stopping only for the occasional coffee and Danish in a cafeteria. It has many grace notes, but does not hold together nearly as well as his first.)

By the Waters of Manhattan is a diptych. Part One tells the story of Sarah Yetta, who emigrated on her own from Russia to the United States and at great personal sacrifice established a family in New York City. In his letters Reznikoff referred to this narrative as his mother's autobiography. It seems that Sarah Reznikoff wrote an account of her life called "Early History of a Seamstress," and her son reworked this material into the first part of *By the Waters of Manhattan*, just as he would later rework the harsh documentary summaries of nineteenth-century American legal cases into the poems that would comprise *Testimony*. And, like a dry run for *Testimony*, oftentimes horrific events, such as serious illness, death, betrayals, pogroms, hostility between family members, and swindles by trusted partners, are told with a deadpan terseness, as vignettes offered up in the no-nonsense manner of oral storytelling: the shocks of fortune laid out and the aftershocks allowed to register in the reader's mind, with no attempt to milk emotion.

The language of this first part has a slightly foreign inflection. The *New York Times* reviewer who panned the book complained: "Too often one feels as if one were reading a jerky and not particularly felicitous translation." The anonymous reviewer was correct to sniff out a "translated" quality in the prose—Reznikoff was channeling his mother's immigrant voice —but wrong to think it was an accident or mistake. Nowadays we are much more aware of the contributions that Jewish–American writers such as Saul Bellow, Bernard Malamud and Philip Roth have made to our literature by twisting and torquing the language and giving it a playful Yiddish tinge. We have also become, I suspect, more grateful to immigrant literature as a whole, whether its source be European, Latin American, Middle-Eastern, African, or Asian, for these priceless accounts of the newcomers's struggles to adapt to the United States. The impatience of the *Times* reviewer in 1930, however, suggests that there was still embarrassment about sounding like a greenhorn. Reznikoff's deliberate cultivation of this alienation-effect in the novel's first part can be read as a stubborn provocation or an entrancing coloration.

The peculiar spin on diction begins with the very title of the novel, *By the Waters of Manhattan.* This title was a favorite of Reznikoff's: he used it repeatedly, almost like a good-luck charm, for a 1929 annual that contained stories, poems, and the first part of the novel; for the 1930 novel; and for his 1962 selected verse. It is hard to say why this phrase held such appeal for him, but I hear in it an echo of Longfellow's *The Song of*

Hiawatha: "By the shores of Gitche Gumee." The locution "By the..." also sounds Biblical (the Old Testament was never far from Reznikoff's mind, and he named two poetry collections, *By the Well of Living and Seeing*). New Yorkers are notorious for disregarding the fact that their city is on the water, so the emphasis on "waters" (plural) suggests an ironic, archaic undertone: in any case, a learned idiom.

Part One ends with a telling line of dialogue, spoken by Sarah Yetta, which operates as a hinge between the two parts: " 'We are a lost generation,' she said. 'It is for our children to do what they can.'" The paradox, for us, is that these first-generation immigrants, who braved dangers so resourcefully and sacrificed so much for their offspring, seem to possess a wholeness of self and spirit, while their relatively more privileged children seem the lost, fragmented ones.

The second part focuses on Sarah's son, Ezekiel, who (we learn from Reznikoff's letters) was not modeled on Reznikoff himself but on his friend Joel. It is significant that this Ezekiel bears the same first name as his grandfather, a *luftmensch* who secretly wrote poetry. When Grandfather Ezekiel died, his wife Hannah burned all his verses, thinking they might contain some reference to nihilists and get the family in trouble with the Russian police. "As she put the first into the fire she said, 'Here's a man's life.'" With characteristic understatement, Reznikoff the novelist leaves it at that; but Reznikoff the man was deeply affected all his life by the burning of his own grandfather's poetic output, an event which actually happened, and his persistence not only in writing, but in seeing the work published at all costs, even setting the type and printing it himself, was clearly in part a defiant response to that earlier erasure. Stephen Fredman makes this point eloquently in his fine study of Reznikoff, *A Menorah for Athena* (University of Chicago Press, 2001).

Here is the primal scene of poetry for Charles Reznikoff. His grandfather's lifework, his secret self, written in Hebrew, language of the Torah—not Yiddish, language of the Diaspora, or Russian, the cosmopolitan language—is destroyed out of fear and ignorance.... This "sad story" was related by Reznikoff obsessively in interviews and in the family histories he wrote in prose and verse.... Making manifest his inheritance, Reznikoff's poems are the great-grandchildren—as though the dead, cremated manuscript had produced, through the intermediary of Charles's mother, this new breed of American Jewish poems.

In the novel, Ezekiel the younger is not a writer, however, but a touchy malcontent, a would-be artist without an art. "If he had studied music, if he could draw and paint..." he broods.

The two parts of the novel are radically different from each other: the first half flows with the folkloric sound of a family chronicle and spans decades, while the second slows down, covers a chronological period of months, and is much more introspective, taking us into Ezekiel's thoughts and stream-of-consciousness. The language in the second part is also different, having lost its foreign tinge and become American-educated, sprinkled with poetic quotations and references to Wordsworth and the Buddha in the Metropolitan Museum. Most crucially, the psychology is vastly different: the first part has an extroverted, indirect psychology, similar to Gertrude Stein's *Three Lives,* where the working-class protagonists are barely aware that they have an unconscious, much less that they are expressing it in every statement they make. Sarah Yetta acts forthrightly and maturely, even as a young girl, with consistent rectitude. She may sorrow at the changeable nature of people's emotions, a neighbor who goes from friendliness to frosty hostility, but she herself is solid and dependable. Ezekiel, her son, is more un-stable in his emotional response, as we see so dramatically and frankly in his sudden satiety with the previously unattainable Jane once she submits erotically to him. Prone to defensive rationalizations, Ezekiel suspects his own motives and is already tired to death of his narcissistic air of superiority, knowing full well he has accomplished so little. (Such neurotic self-suspicion would have been a luxury for his mother, who needed to hold onto any shred of self-respect in the face of a community that denounced her as prideful when she struck out on her own.)

Thematically, the two parts connect to each other with an organic rightness, telling the whole painful story of immigra-tion in America as it has tended to play out on the family front. Still, the halves are in many ways radically unlike: so it is puz-zling that both the novel's defenders and detractors paid so little attention, in 1930, to the differences between the two parts, thereby scanting the book's haunting strangeness.

When first published by Boni, it contained an introduction by the then-prominent literary figure Louis Untermeyer. He began his introduction by saying: "It is a long time since I have read a story so obviously sincere—and so tellingly simple. The simplicity, from the first paragraph to the last, is not an inci-dental virtue or a trick of technique; it is essential. It bears no relation to the over-cultivated monosyllables which have come as a reaction to our over-cultivated (and belated) Eighteen Nineties. Here is nothing falsely *naïf* in story or in style. There is, in fact, no 'style.'" Though Untermeyer goes on to praise the novel for its severe refusal of romantic theatricality, and for the realism of its inconclusive ending, I am struck by the appli-cation of this backhanded-compliment critical vocabulary ("simple," "sincere," "no 'style'") to Reznikoff.

The great critic Lionel Trilling, who also praised the novel in a glowing review that appeared in *The Menorah Journal,* was similarly taken with Reznikoff's sincerity and purity: "Certainly it is not great prose in the sense that it is exciting or compelling. It makes no pretension to this. Perhaps it is merely such prose as we should expect at the least from every writer—each word understood and in its right place; each word saying exactly what it should say and not forced beyond its meaning.... In short, style becomes its writer's morality.... The charm of Mr. Reznikoff's book lies in its avoidance of ... falsification. His book has true words, hence truth—solid, raw, sociological truth."

This is a splendid tribute, but I wonder if such points of view have not done Reznikoff's literary reputation more harm than good. To make of Reznikoff an angel of sincerity and raw sociological truth-telling seems to me to slight the selectivity of his artistry and the lyrical beauty of his language. Let us consider some examples:

> He was glad to find himself on the bridge, the tenements and office buildings behind him, his face towards the sky. Soon the roadway changed to slats of wood, springy under his feet after so many miles of asphalt. Ezekiel was pleased, too, after the even curves of gutters and the straight lines of pavements and houses to see the free glitter of the water. He was now in the rhythm of walking, that sober dance which despite all the dances man knows, he dances most.

No "style"? Reznikoff speaks enthusiastically of "a new science, citycraft," and his novel is replete with urban tableaux that offer up the verbal equivalent of Sloan's or Hopper's New York paintings, like the marvelous descriptions of the Automat or the barber shop or the Italian procession. There are astute little aphorisms dropped into the text: "Somewhere there must be a woman—so a girl, he thought, dreams of the man she hopes to marry and at last puts up with her husband." Or: "He decided not to drink. After a while his thirst would pass, as it often did, just like hunger and cold. The body, he had found, makes its needs known and after awhile, unanswered, concludes its master cannot satisfy it, though he would, or is busy, and courteously becomes silent." This is lucid, spare writing, yes, but style-less? I find it elegant.

There is also a richness of sensory description, the way a character tries to shake off "his familiar despondency" and adhere to the available charms of the present. "In the bright morning he looked eagerly at the houses, at each horse and milkwagon...." "The silver of the thin dime was an unexpected pleasure." "How good to rest." "He ate slowly, to taste each morsel to the utmost, and praised God." This elemental side of Reznikoff most resembles his contemporary William Carlos Williams, who ended a poem about a beggar-woman eating in the street: "Food, the great comforter."

If the novel ends inconclusively, it is because Ezekiel's hopefulness and discouragement have fought to a legitimate standstill. He has managed to start his own business, a bookstore in Greenwich Village, with virtually no capital, though now he has little time for an inner life and feels imprisoned, tied down to work; he has shaken off virginity and has a robust sex-life, though now he is growing tired of his mistress; he decides one moment to drink "the bitter night of his life," and the next moment is diverted by a girl passing by; he looks at himself and sees both an ordinary young man and a swindler. He is, in Reznikoff's words, "Janus-faced," turning one visage to the world and another away from it. He lives on a knife-edge between optimism and despondency. Just when everything seems depleted inside, there is an upturn. This bobbing-up reflex in the midst of potentially drowning is a deeply moving trope in Reznikoff's prose and verse, he reverts to it again and again, as his way of bearing witness to the human spirit's resiliency within a punishing world. "It seemed to Ezekiel that his thoughts at last brought out the sun, whose brightness they had been touching and leaving and returning to, as a bird pecks at a golden fruit." The power of one man's thought to bring out the sun—that is true magic, an indication of why *By the Waters of Manhattan* is finally a poet's novel.

PART ONE

EZEKIEL AND HANNAH VOLSKY lived in Baron Chichiroshan's courtyard in the city of Elizavetgrad, Russia—in a bedroom, living-room, and kitchen in the outhouse. Near them flowed the Ingul. Their children had a large garden to play in, and there the baron's son, Peter, often played with them. The baron liked Israel, the younger boy. He called him "the little rabbi" and gave him a fur hat and some of Peter's old clothes.

That summer was a happy one for Michael—the elder boy—Israel, and Sarah Yetta. They spent the days looking for berries and flowers in the garden. (How she wanted to go to school like her friends, books under her arm; she asked her father again and again, "When am I going to go to school?")

In winter Ezekiel took sick. The children walked about on tiptoe. The house was cold and the windows covered with ice. It was a long time before he was well. And then one evening he told Hannah that his employer would keep him only if he worked Saturdays. (Ezekiel was a bookkeeper.) The employer's nephew had just come from Switzerland—and he was put in Ezekiel's place.

Hyam came to their house at the feast of Purim, and Ezekiel listened to him with great interest. Next day Ezekiel and Hannah packed up everything. Late in the afternoon two sleds came to their door. On one the furniture was put, on the other cushions and quilts for them to sit on. They left the courtyard and the garden where the children had been so happy. Everybody was saying good-by. Sarah Yetta cried, but her father smiled and told her that they were going to a wonderful country.

They were going to a village called Snamenka. The horses were good and went swiftly. It wasn't long before Sarah Yetta was dizzy and so were her mother and the other children. Soon not a house was to be seen, only white snow and blue sky.

When Sarah Yetta awoke she was in a large room. Her mother's bed stood in a corner; on it were piled their feather-beds and pillows. Between the two windows toward the street were their big table and their benches. On the other side of the room was the chest in which Hannah kept her trousseau. Near the brick oven was the kitchen table.

Sarah Yetta's head hurt. Her mother tied a wet handkerchief about it, and Sarah Yetta dressed and went to one of the windows. The houses were not close together; they were only one story high and had straw roofs. From the chimneys heavy smoke was rising. The women that passed had colored handkerchiefs about their heads. Sarah Yetta ran to her mother and cried, "Everybody has a headache in this awful country!" Hannah kissed her and explained that it was the headdress of the women in Snamenka. She went back to the window and watched the wide street. Many cows and horses passed, and the people looked healthy and strong.

After supper Ezekiel gave the children their first lesson. Israel and Sarah Yetta took to the lessons cheerfully, but Michael was dull. In the city he had been sent to the school of a teacher who struck him on the head and made him deaf. This teacher became known as Berele "Knock-'em-down." (At last he killed a boy and was sent to Siberia.) Ezekiel would explain and explain the lessons to Michael—and sink back in his chair and say, "It is worse than if he were killed."

One day Ezekiel came home with the man who had been in their house in Elizavetgrad at the feast of Purim. They sat up until late at night. When Hyam was gone, Ezekiel looked sad. Long afterwards, Sarah Yetta understood why they had moved to Snamenka and why her father was so discouraged. Seven years before, the first railway had been built through Snamenka, and the contractors of supplies soon became rich. A second railway was planned, but it turned out to be just a few miles long and there was no chance for Ezekiel to make money as a contractor.

He had to make a living, somehow, and was advised to become a glazier: many windows would be needed for the railway cars. Ezekiel had a friend in Elizavetgrad who sold glaziers' supplies, and went there to learn the trade. Hannah and the children were left in Snamenka. She used to cheer them up by telling them stories and playing with them, but Sarah Yetta often found her crying at her work.

One night Sarah Yetta could not sleep and lay watching her mother. She was doing some patching by candlelight and as Sarah Yetta saw the tears falling from her mother's eyes she turned to the pillow and cried, too. When she woke, it was still night. Her father sat at the table with her mother. He had brought his father to Snamenka. Her grandfather walked about saying his prayers. When he had finished, he asked his daughter-in-law how she was. Hannah answered that she would be well if business were better. Her father-in-law looked at her sternly and said, "A good Jewess does not complain, but is thankful and satisfied no matter how business is."

"That is all very well for a man to say when his children are provided for, but what shall I do here in a wilderness with my boys and no schools? How can I be satisfied?"

"If they are to be great, they will be great even if they are brought up in a wilderness," her father-in-law answered. "I have two sons. I wanted them to be rabbis and I hired the best teachers in the city for them. I also had two nephews of mine, orphans, brought up in my house. I made one of them a tailor and the other a capmaker. One of them is now rich. He has horses and carriages, and your Ezekiel hasn't a penny to his name."

Ezekiel spoke for the first time. "That is your fault."

His father turned on him. "What do you mean?"

He smiled. "Oh, you took such care of your store and house that you made me a beggar."

His father answered, "God wanted it so."

"God had no more to do with it than I had. He has more to do than to watch over you and see that you don't sign a blank deed and let Spectorov the Usurer take your house away."

His father took a few sips of tea and said, "You always were an unbeliever."

"Unbeliever!" Ezekiel cried. "How can I believe in such things? A man takes away your property in broad daylight and because he prays three times a day you don't try to get it back!"

"How can I get it back? How can I profane the name of God by bringing my claim to gentiles? Do you think I'll send a Jew to Siberia in my old age?"

"What are you afraid of? Why isn't he afraid of Siberia?" But Hannah begged her husband to say no more.

In the morning their grandfather, Fivel Volsky, looked carefully at the boys and then at Sarah Yetta. "Ai, ai, ai, what is the matter with Sarah Yetta's eyes?" he asked.

"When Ezekiel was so sick last winter," her mother said, "the children had the measles. They had it lightly. I didn't bother much with them; I had my hands full with Ezekiel.

While she was sick, Sarah Yetta went off to a neighbor's house; of course, they brought her right back, but it was too late. She was almost blind for a year. She is better now."

"You'll have to see to her eyes. This is very bad for a girl."

At twelve o'clock the white cloth was taken off the table, and their grandfather began to teach the children. They found the beginning of the Bible very interesting. The house now became lively. Three other boys and a little girl, Sarah Yetta's age, came to be taught by the grandfather.

Ezekiel Volsky had brought from Elizavetgrad a case of glass and a glass-cutter with a diamond point. His father was to teach the children so that he could give all of his time to his work. But the new cars came with windows set, and glaziers were sent from Great Russia to do what work there was.

He did a little business in the village as an agent for dealers in wheat. He also worked at winnowing. He was not paid in money, but with chickens, eggs, flour, flaxseed, and other things. The work did not please him. He saw no future for his boys in the village. He would argue with his father again and again about the house and store that had been his father's, and they would both lose their tempers. Hannah would say to Ezekiel, "You ought not to speak that way before the children. It cannot be helped. Why aggravate yourself and him?"

He would answer, "I cannot keep still. He has beggared me."

Afterwards, Sarah Yetta learned the story of her grandfather's house and store. Her great-grandfather, Israel Volsky, was rich. He had an inn in Zezonova and a dress-goods store in Elizavetgrad. On the boulevard in Elizavetgrad he had a double house with an iron roof. Her grandfather was his only son. Fivel prayed and studied holy books all day, and his father was happy to have so pious a son.

But when her great-grandfather died, her grandfather had to take care of the business. She did not know what became of the inn, but to run a store like Fivel Volsky became a proverb in Elizavetgrad. A man would come to him and say, "I have four grown daughters and you have a store full of goods. I don't know what to do: I have no money and they have nothing to wear." Her grandfather would write an order on the store that the man be given what his daughters needed. Fivel's wife would complain, but he would say, "I am only God's cashier. When people are going about barefoot and hungry, am I to hide His money?"

Then a fire broke out and all the stores were burned down. (In those days nobody in Elizavetgrad was insured.) The other merchants failed and did not pay their notes; Fivel paid everybody and was left without money.

However, he still had his house. He rented half of it to Moses Spectorov. Spectorov's younger son was a law student. One day gypsies and peasants had a fight in the street. Spectorov and his son asked Fivel if he had seen the fight. He had. "The police are asking us for the names of those who have seen it. Will you sign this?" and they gave him a blank to sign. Fivel did not think that Spectorov who seemed so pious was a swindler. Fivel's elder son had married into a family of another town and lived there. The younger, Ezekiel, was in hiding until someone was hired to be a soldier in his place. He married then, and came to Elizavetgrad to live in the part of the house Spectorov had; but Spectorov told him that the house had not been his father's for five years.

When Fivel heard that Spectorov would be sent to Siberia for forging the deed, he would not bring the charge against him. "I cannot send a Jew in a gaberdine to prison," he said to his son. "You can live without this house. The world is big, and God is great. He will take care of you."

Ezekiel was not so easily content to be penniless. "I am not supposed to provide you with riches," his father said. "I was to provide you with learning and to teach you to be upright. That I did." Spectorov did not stay in the house long. He sold it to a priest and moved to another part of the town.

Ezekiel Volsky had no money to move from Snamenka. He moved to a house near the railway. The tracks were on a high embankment, and whenever a train went by, the children ran to look up at it. In a hollow in front of the house was a brook and their well. They had a big yard, and their door was big and heavy. To the left of the hall was a large storeroom, and to the right, another large room: this had four windows, two toward the yard, two toward the street, and in this room they cooked, ate, slept, worked, and studied.

Grandfather Fivel would sit at the head of the long table, wearing a black skullcap, a black quilted jacket, black sateen knickerbockers, white woolen stockings, and black slippers. At his right sat Jacob, the son of the richest Jew in the village, and three other boys; on the other bench were his grandsons, Michael and Israel, and last, the blacksmith's son.

"Israel, why aren't you studying?" his grandfather said.

"I am hungry."

"You just ate. Everyone ate when you did, and no one is hungry but you."

"What did I have? Just a piece of stale rye bread."

"You ought to thank God for that," his grandfather said angrily. Then he turned to Jacob, "What did you have?"

Jacob pulled a long face and to please Israel's grandfather answered, "Soup with just one noodle"—the children burst out laughing—"and roast goose and—"

"He stuffed himself," Grandfather Fivel said. "Today is Thursday, and he doesn't know his lesson yet. Is it good to eat so much?"

Hannah and Sarah Yetta were sitting with their backs to the oven. Sarah Yetta was making lace and had finished her sixth piece. Her mother was patching underwear. "I can see right through them," she said. "There's no place for more patches; it's all holes."

Her eyes were red. "Why are you crying, Mamma?" Sarah Yetta asked.

"I was thinking of a song about a woman who has no money to buy anything for her children and whose brothers have forgotten her."

"If parents would educate their daughters, sisters could write to their brothers. Mamma, if you wrote to your brothers, they would surely help you."

Hannah looked up from her sewing and said, "My child, no one can help us but God."

"Yes," Sarah Yetta said, "I remember that in the story of Noah's ark the bird brings an olive leaf to show that a bitter leaf from God is better than a sweet one from man."

"Man helps a great deal, but it comes to little." Then, turning to Grandfather Fivel, Hannah said, "Did you hear what Sarah Yetta said about the dove and the bitter leaf?"

Grandfather Fivel came over to them. "She has her father's brains. But he did not want to study the Torah—only languages." Grandfather Fivel put on his coat. "It is going to be very cold."

"Why shouldn't one study languages?" Sarah Yetta said. "King Solomon knew a great many."

Her grandfather looked at her. "She compares herself to King Solomon. I wanted her father to be a rabbi, but he studied languages instead. What good did they do him?"

Sarah Yetta had finished all the lace. "Bring it to Katrina," her mother said, "and ask for flour and potatoes. The children didn't have enough for dinner, and there is nothing for supper." Katrina was marrying off her daughter, and the lace was for the bride's towels. "Look at the frost on the window and Papa isn't home. It is so cold I don't see how he will ride through the fields."

Grandfather Fivel sent Michael to fetch water. The other children ran out gleefully to slide on the ice. Wrapped in her mother's striped shawl, Sarah Yetta went to Katrina and came back with potatoes, flour, and a dozen eggs.

Her mother looked at the potatoes. "My, my, they are as small as hazel nuts. What am I to do with them? And I cannot make noodles out of the flour—it is rye. Grandpa must have something warm and filling tonight. He is fasting today."

Sarah Yetta and her mother peeled the potatoes to make soup. Grandfather Fivel was saying the afternoon prayers. The children ran in and shouted, "A train full of soldiers with beards went by. The people say they are taking men over thirty to the army." (The Russians were at war with the Turks.)

Grandfather Fivel said, "Keep quiet now. Go back to your studies." They went to their seats and took up their pencils.

They heard Ezekiel in the yard. He and another man came in, their faces covered with snow. They carried sacks of flour and potatoes.

Hannah and Ezekiel whispered together. Sarah Yetta could see that they were worried and asked what the trouble was. Her father said with a smile, "A little girl should not know everything."

Hannah went to the chest and took out her silk coat. Ezekiel put it under his arm, and he and the other man left the house. Grandfather Fivel told Michael to put up the samovar and the others to go home. "Come a little later tomorrow," he said.

Ezekiel came back with a middle-aged woman, Dobrosh. She took off her big fur coat and the galoshes over her felt shoes. She had on a blue and red checked dress and had a red handkerchief about her ruddy, good-natured face. Dobrosh told Hannah to lie down and rest and began to work about the house. Hannah drew the curtains of her bed. The table was set, and the others had tea. Ezekiel had supper with the children and then said, "All will have to go to bed now. We will not study tonight. Mamma does not feel well, and the house must be quiet."

The others went to sleep above the oven, but Sarah Yetta's head would ache when she slept in a warm place. So she pushed the benches together and put a featherbed on them. When she woke, her father and grandfather were saying the morning prayers. Dobrosh was kneading dough. Sarah Yetta was wondering at a chicken—ready for the pot—on their table, and thinking of her mother's pawned coat, when she heard a strange cry. She looked about. Her father and grandfather saw her and both said, "*Mazel tov* (good luck), you have a little sister." Dobrosh went to the bed and brought out the baby on a pillow.

"Oo, what a dark little thing she is."

Grandfather Fivel smiled. "Don't worry. She'll be a better looking girl than you."

Her father said, "Now go back to bed. It's too early for you to be up."

"But I must study my lesson," Sarah Yetta said.

Her grandfather said, "I wish the boys were as anxious to study—and she with her blind eyes needs it badly."

Ezekiel was helping Sarah Yetta with her lesson, when in came their landlord's son. His hat and coat were of Persian lamb. Now he had long icicles in his mustache and beard. "Where are you coming from so early, Antushka?" Ezekiel asked.

Antushka took off his hat, untied the belt of his coat, and shook off the snow. He wore a red blouse with a beaded girdle and had on black leather boots. He sat down and began to cry. "What is it, Antushka?" Ezekiel asked.

Antushka wiped his eyes on the leather cuffs of his coat. "I just brought my younger brother to the army. I cannot go back to the house because of his wife. How can I face her? Their baby is only two weeks old. Ah, brothers, brothers," and he began to sob.

They all had tea. The sun rose. Antushka and Ezekiel went away. Dobrosh waited on Hannah. At two o'clock the children were sent home and the table set for the Sabbath. Dobrosh asked Grandfather Fivel how her grandson Jacob was getting on. Grandfather Fivel said, "I don't know what to do with him. He is like my grandson Michael. A teacher hit Michael on one ear so that blood came out of the other. Since then he can't hear well. God knows what he'll grow up to be. But Jacob was born stupid." New straw was brought in for the floor. Dobrosh put two loaves of white bread on the table and the candles were lit.

In the morning, when it was still dark, they heard a tapping at a window. It was Simon Rubinov, Grandfather Fivel's nephew. He had just moved to Snamenka to go into business with his wife's uncle.

Ezekiel, Fivel, and Simon had much to talk about, and then Simon said to Fivel, "Uncle, you will have to teach my eldest son, Saul."

"How old is he?" Fivel asked.

"Six. I'd like to have Saul stay here."

Grandfather Fivel told him he could bring his son in two weeks. Hannah would be out of bed then.

A few weeks later Hannah went for her first walk. Grandfather Fivel watched the children writing, and Sarah Yetta took care of the baby. She began a lullaby. Her grandfather turned to her and said, "You sing well, but you ought to know that a woman ought not to sing before men." He pointed to the children and smiled.

"A little while ago we were taught that Miriam sang and danced before the Israelites."

"That was different. They had just crossed the Red Sea. Besides, now we are in exile."

Hannah came in, followed by a boy with a bag of flour. Her father-in-law looked at her, surprised. She sat down and sighed.

"What are you going to do?" he asked.

"I am going to bake rolls. I have two customers already."

"What do you mean? You have six children and the house to take care of." (She had two sons, Mordecai and Abram, younger than Israel.)

"Father," she said, "I haven't much to do, and I must help Ezekiel. He is not strong and has eight to support. How can he do that, especially when he is just learning a trade? Besides, maybe I'll be able to help him educate the children."

"God will help."

Hannah shook her head. "My father believes that when you work, God helps you. He does not believe in miracles."

Saul Rubinov had been with the Volskys two weeks when his mother asked, "How is my big boy?"

Hannah said, "He's a nice boy and has a good head on his shoulders, but you ought to dress him properly. Make him a coat and trousers like those of my boys. His shirt sticks out of his rompers, and the children can't help pulling it."

Saul's mother went on to complain about how much she had to do. She was annoyed at what Hannah had said and after that called the Volskys "the beggarly aristocrats" and "the proud beggars."

One day a train crowded with soldiers stopped at the village. Soldiers were billeted in each house, in some as many as twelve. In Ezekiel's house the soldiers asked them to put up the samovar and were happy at seeing the fresh rolls. A soldier with a big blond beard lifted Sarah Yetta in his arms. The tears rolled down his cheeks, and he said, "I left a little girl like you at home."

The soldiers gathered about the table and were very jolly. But one, a Jew, stood facing the wall and prayed. Hannah found out from the others that he was fasting—his gun was lost. The soldiers said he would be shot for losing his gun in time of war.

His father and wife waited impatiently for Ezekiel. In the morning Sarah Yetta found her father still in bed and her grandfather walking about, very happy. She asked him about the soldier who had lost his gun. "The Jews of the village each gave some money, and Father went to Elizavetgrad and bought a gun. He came back at three o'clock and the soldiers left at five."

There were Jews in Snamenka poorer than the Volskys. A landowner gave one three roubles to kiss a red-hot poker. His family was without food and the Passover holidays near—so he did.

Some of the landowners were friendly to Ezekiel. He played chess with them, and they sent him presents of food. Once a rich peasant came to his house for a lesson in manners. When the serfs were freed, Marko Prokopenko's father bought the estate of a spendthrift nobleman. Marko no longer wore the peasant dress; good-natured and intelligent, he gave his children a good education. Afterwards, he built a power-mill in Elizavetgrad, and though his flour was of poor quality, it was the cheapest. On the day he came, Ezekiel left word that none of the children should be at home. He was afraid that they would laugh at Marko. Ezekiel taught him how to hold his saucer and how to drink tea from it without too much noise. For this, Marko sent him six fat hens and a rooster. The rooster was so big he could eat off the table. They had to keep the chickens in the house away from the dogs. His father sneered at Ezekiel: he took his hat off when he ate with Marko. But Hannah said that her father had said it was only a custom for Jews to eat with their hats on, not a law.

Next spring Ezekiel bought a horse and wagon and drove about the countryside as a glazier. He came back from a trip to tell Hannah of a man who wanted her to run one of his taverns. It was in a small village; but a learned man was there to teach the boys, their living quarters would be free, and what they could make on the fish, rolls, and dumplings sold would be theirs.

Hannah was anxious to leave Snamenka. Their neighbor, Homa Ivanovitch, had married his only daughter to his servant. Homa Ivanovitch's granddaughter, Danilka, was Sarah Yetta's age and they played together. She was once in his house playing with Danilka, when Danilka's father urged Sarah Yetta to become a Christian.

"Why?" she asked.

"To have a better god."

"What god?"

He pointed to the ikon covered with cobwebs and dead flies. "Why, that god," she said, "can't even chase a dead fly away."

He threw her out of the house and would have followed to beat her, if his father-in-law had not stopped him. "Why do you argue with children?" she heard Homa Ivanovitch say.

One midnight Danilka's father brought a bag of wheat. "If you'll bring it in the daytime, I'll buy it," Ezekiel said.

Danilka's father became angry. "Do you think it isn't mine?"

"Well, then," said Ezekiel, "there's no reason why you can't bring it in the daytime," and would not buy it.

Since then Danilka's father had a grudge against the Volskys. Whenever Ezekiel was not home, he would throw stones at their door. One night he threw a stone, and they were waiting for more to follow, but none did. They looked through the shutters and saw the sky bright above them. They thought he had set fire to the house and ran out. Then they saw that the town was burning, and the church bells began to ring.

The fire burned for three days, first on the west side and then on the east. After it was over Danilka's father came quietly into their house and sat down. Grandfather Fivel said to him, "You were the first to see the fire."

"How do you know?" he asked. Since then Hannah was afraid of him.

A wagon came for the Volskys, they packed their things, and left Snamenka gladly. Grandfather Fivel stayed behind until a new teacher would come. Hannah made the tavern neat and clean. So good was her food that the neighboring villages soon heard of it. In a few weeks Ezekiel went away and left his wife happy: she worked hard, but the business was going nicely.

Business became so good that she had to hire a woman to help her. And then, one day, in came the owner's wife with a constable and served Hannah with a notice to vacate: she was taking trade away from the tavern the owner's wife ran. Hannah had to leave that day. The owner's wife was afraid that if the peasants found out why Hannah was going they would make trouble, and she had a wagon ready. What could Hannah do? She packed up her belongings, and she and the children went to Elizavetgrad.

* * *

Hannah's father, Benjamin Hirsh Venitsky, was not at home. He had gone to tutor a young man to be a rabbi and was to stay away a year. Her stepmother and little sister were living in one room. (Hannah's stepmother had no children. Ezekiel was her cousin, and she loved him like a son.) Before Benjamin Hirsh left home, he bought his wife a stall in the marketplace and there she sold beans, dried peas, and cereals. She welcomed Ezekiel's wife and children with open arms, and her landlady made room for them.

In the five years they had been away, Elizavetgrad had grown greatly. But instead of spreading out, the people huddled together and even lived in cellars; and the rent for these was high and none to be had. Hannah did not want to stay in Elizavetgrad. There was no place for the children to play, the air in the crowded rooms and streets was bad, and she was afraid they would become sickly. Besides, she would be unable to help her husband. All the business was done at the marketplace. That was far off, and she could not leave the children alone just yet. But her stepmother urged her to stay for the sake of the boys' education.

In three weeks Ezekiel came, and Hannah and he decided to move to a small town, Dmitrovka. Ezekiel knew the town well: he had worked for landowners in the neighborhood. Dmitrovka had a free Hebrew school. Grandfather Fivel would not have to teach the boys. He was now living with his other son, Abram Loeb; there he had more comforts than Ezekiel could give him.

Meanwhile, Sarah Yetta found out that life with her mother's stepmother would be unbearable. Sarah Yetta loved to read, but her mother's stepmother thought a girl should only do housework and sew: at ten she was a young lady, and at fifteen she was to be married off. One day her mother's stepmother found Sarah Yetta reading—a Russian book at that. How her mother's stepmother carried on! Books were men's affairs, and if Sarah Yetta would stop meddling with what did not concern her, she would have pretty dresses and whatever she wished. Sarah Yetta answered that what she wished for most was paper and books and at least one lesson a week. Her stepmother told Hannah how spoiled Sarah Yetta was. Sarah Yetta asked her mother why women should be against educating girls. She answered that all elderly people thought that if women would read they would not do their household duties.

"Do you remember when Grandfather Fivel gave me *The Tree of Life* to read and memorize? In that it said, 'He who does not know how to read is blind.'"

"A man is meant," Hannah answered.

"I don't believe intelligent people think a woman is not as good as a man." And Sarah Yetta made up her mind not to listen to her mother or her mother's stepmother and to learn as much as she could.

In the autumn the Volskys moved to Dmitrovka. There they lived opposite a park. The houses of Dmitrovka were built far apart and each had a garden and many trees. Hannah gave birth to another boy. The boys—those old enough—went to school, and Ezekiel managed to make a living.

Grandfather Fivel came to see them in the spring. He complained about the way his other son, Abram Loeb, was bringing up his children. Abram Loeb's wife was a bad stepmother: she did not care if the children were taught or not. Sarah Yetta told her grandfather how she missed him. He said that he missed them too, but it was his duty to stay with her motherless cousins and see that they were brought up decently. Then he quoted an old saying, "When the mother is dead, the father is blind." Grandfather Fivel enjoyed his stay. He called Sarah

Yetta's sister "a little Greek girl"—she was dark and beautiful. Though she was only two years old, she danced and sang.

At the end of spring Ezekiel went to Nikolaiev. Two weeks went by and his family did not hear from him. They had only a bag of flour. "Will you be able to sell rolls in the market?" Hannah asked Sarah Yetta, and baked a hundred rolls.

Sarah Yetta had a neat dress and wore shoes and stockings. When she found a place in the bakers' row, they made fun of her and chased her away. "What kind of an aristocrat is this?" they said. She wandered about with her rolls, wondering what to do.

She went to a store where they had bought flour and told the owner how she had been chased from the bakers' row. She asked him to let her stand near his steps. There she spread her tablecloth and put out the rolls. A crowd gathered: the sight of a white tablecloth under the rolls was unusual, and in a little while they were sold. People asked her who her parents were, and Abram Sinkovsky, the owner of the store, said he would send them a two-hundred-pound sack of flour. She told him that her father was not at home and that they could not pay for it just then; but he answered that she was not to worry about that.

Hannah baked rolls three times a day. Israel was taken from school and sent in Sarah Yetta's place to the market—she had to help at home. Though he was not quite ten years old, Israel was an old hand at selling. He had been selling matches and salt since he was seven.

All that his family had from Ezekiel were hopeful letters, but no money. They wrote him that they were getting along nicely. One afternoon a carriage rolled up to their door and a short, stout, well-dressed man came into the house. He had just come from Nikolaiev. He gave Hannah twenty-five roubles that her husband had sent and told them how Ezekiel had struggled until he found work. "It's hard without money to find something to do in a strange place," he said. He lived just around the corner and made Hannah promise to come to tea and meet his wife.

Hannah found time to go. He had three sons and three daughters. "They will come to see us," Hannah said. Eva was Sarah Yetta's age and she asked at once, "Does Eva go to school?" School was all Sarah Yetta thought about. Many and many a time when no one would see her, she would cry because she could not go to school.

"She is given lessons at home," her mother answered. Three of the children did come the next day, among them Eva. They told Sarah Yetta and her mother that their mother was dead. Their stepmother had refurnished the house and had hired a teacher for them. She also wanted the youngest boy to take lessons on the violin. She thought it dreadful to go about barefoot. Hannah told them that she must be a fine woman: there were stepmothers who did not think that their stepchildren should be educated. They said that they appreciated what she was doing, but it was hard for them.

Eva asked Sarah Yetta to one of the lessons. They did not seem to care for it and fooled about with their teacher. Their stepmother came in and told Eva she need not study anymore that day, but could play with Sarah Yetta. Eva laughed and said, "She does not play. All her time is taken up with reading and sewing."

"Little girls should have some fun, too," her stepmother said.

In a few weeks Ezekiel came home. He brought them all presents. Israel was given a pair of boots with red tops. He hung them on a tree in the woods and then could not find the tree.

His father asked him why he had not brought the boots home and then gone back to play.

"We were playing soldiers. I was the general. If I went away," he said earnestly, "my men would be captured."

They went on with their baking: times were bad. Next spring the landlord made them move. He said that they baked so much the house would catch on fire.

Hannah had an abscess in her throat. She was afraid to trust herself to the doctors in Dmitrovka and went to Elizavetgrad. Sarah Yetta was to take care of the house and do the cooking.

In a few days she ran out of bread. She set about to bake a sort of biscuit they ate. She made the dough and then tried to heat the oven. They used dried manure for fuel and she put in as much as she had seen her mother use. Then she placed two pots of water inside to keep the flames from the chimney. When she set a match to the manure, it burst into a great blaze. She had not realized that because of the long season of dry weather, the manure was so dry. She ran outside and watched the sparks flying out of the chimney over the straw roof. After a while they became less, and she went into the house to find the fire in the oven dying down. She put the dough in, her hands trembling for excitement. Then she began to worry that the chimney was on fire. She took two pails of water and some sacks and climbed to the attic. She soaked the sacks and put them on the chimney. They became dry almost at once. She was sure now that there was danger of a fire. She wet the sacks again and again until they no longer dried on the chimney. She was looking about for a place to lean against and rest, when she saw what seemed a man hanging from the ceiling. Their landlord's grandfather had hanged himself in this attic. That is why we were able to rent the house—no one else would live here, she thought, and slid down the ladder. When she opened her eyes, her brothers were about her. She remembered the biscuits; they must be burnt black, she thought, and ran to the oven door. Ugh! Inside she found white, cold lumps of dough.

Later, Sarah Yetta saw their landlord and told him that she had seen his grandfather hanging in the attic. He called her all kinds of ugly names, but quickly went up with her. What she had seen was a sack of dried apples, and she felt such a fool.

Next day she was sick. Israel woke her chanting the Psalms. It seemed to her that he said them even better than her father, and she cried as she listened. When he had finished, she said, "Israel, I'll not be able to make anything today. I cannot start a fire. We'll just have to buy bread and milk and live on that until Mamma comes back."

He answered cheerfully, "Don't worry. I'm going to market now to sell my matches, and then I'll bring some bread."

Hannah came back, pale and sick. Sarah Yetta hugged her and kissed her and told her all that had happened. She wrung her hands and cried, "The child might have been burned to death!"

Soon their life went on as before. It disgusted Sarah Yetta. Her mind was starving. She loved to read, but how could she when she had so much to do? She was too miserable to eat and wished to die.

One night she woke and saw that her father had come. She would have risen from bed and gone to him—he had not been home a long time—but she heard her name. Her father sat at the head of the table. The light shone full on his face, on his high white forehead and long black beard. In Snamenka they had nicknamed him "Ezekiel-with-the-long-beard." Sarah Yetta could not see her mother, but she heard her telling him about her. When he heard that Sarah Yetta was so unhappy and wished to die, he repeated after her mother, "She is unhappy," and hid his face in his handkerchief; Sarah Yetta was shocked to see him cry.

Then she heard her mother say, "What can we do? We cannot send her to school. I need her at home: I have no other help."

In the morning the children all greeted their father and hurried to their work. Sarah Yetta said nothing about the night before and neither did her mother or father. In the evening, Ezekiel told them how he had worked in the house of Judge Kormazine, a great and good man. He had spoken to Ezekiel about the Jews. Their life was going to be hard, he said. In some places the priests had been ordered to preach against them. The Judge thought that the Jews ought to change their way of living: they ought to learn trades and professions and give up being merchants and middlemen. But, of course, as long as the government would allow only a few Jews in the colleges, only the rich could become professional men.

"In a home where there are stepchildren," their father said, "everyone is treated alike as long as all goes well. But when things go wrong and food is scarce, who is treated badly?"

"The stepchildren," they answered.

"That is what is happening in Russia now. The Jews are considered the stepchildren of the country. When things run smoothly, they are let alone; but as soon as there is trouble, they are oppressed. The stepchildren must be much better than the others not to be blamed.

"To show how falsehoods about the Jews spread, Judge Kormazine told me of a case he had. A peasant woman came to the fair with two bulls. A Jew gave her sixty roubles for them, and then the woman cried out she had not been paid. A crowd gathered, and the Jew and the peasant woman were taken to Judge Kormazine. The Jew said he had brought eighty roubles to the fair, he had paid sixty for the bulls and had twenty left. These he showed to the Judge. The woman kept saying that the Jew had not paid her. He had seen the money she had and that was what he said he had paid for the bulls. The Judge looked at the Jew's money and said it was counterfeit. Then he asked for the peasant woman's money and said that was counterfeit, too. She fell on her knees and confessed she had it from the Jew. The Judge asked her why she had accused the Jew falsely. She answered that times were bad and she had taxes to pay; she thought it would not matter if she took money from a Jew—the Jews had plenty. There were riots in a number of taverns in the town before the truth was known. And by that time most of the peasants had left for home with the story of how a Jew had tried to cheat a peasant woman out of her bulls.

"'Each Jew,' the Judge concluded, 'must try to overcome the feeling against Jews by his own work and life.'"

Sarah Yetta was thinking of what the Judge had said about Jews learning trades and said, "Father, would you apprentice Israel to a shoemaker or a tailor?"

Ezekiel answered, "I should not like a child of mine to be a shoemaker or a tailor. The ignorant people of the town have done this work for generations. When a family has a stupid or a bad child, they apprentice him to one of these trades; and so they have become the trades of the stupid. In the cities, they are in somewhat better hands, but, still, a tailor's apprentice must wait four or five years before he is allowed to use the needle. In the meantime, he has to bring water for his employer and mind the children."

Then Ezekiel turned to Sarah Yetta and said, "Little girl, you were born into the wrong family with your ideas." She became red. "You were born the eldest girl, and this family needs your help badly. We are lucky to have you here to help your mother;

otherwise, she could not go on as she does. You can read and write. Many Jewish girls of well-to-do families cannot do that. You are also handy with the needle. Now you must make plans to suit your circumstances. Learn as much as you can, but we could not send you to school, even if we were better off, because you are needed at home."

In the winter Hannah gave birth to another boy. The day after Easter, she went to market with her rolls, and Ezekiel went out on business. They soon came back—there had been a pogrom in Elizavetgrad and everybody was saying that there would be others throughout Russia. Hannah was crying because her parents were in Elizavetgrad. In Dmitrovka the gentiles called a meeting and resolved to defend the Jews against rioters. They sent word to the Jews not to be afraid; however, should soldiers come, they added, they could do nothing. In a few days Ezekiel went to Elizavetgrad and found Hannah's parents robbed, but safe.

That summer was a hard one, especially for Jews. They had no spirit to do anything. In the autumn diphtheria broke out, and in Dmitrovka about three hundred children died every week. Luckily, none of Ezekiel and Hannah's children had it. In the winter there was smallpox in town. Their baby, Fishel, caught it and was sick for eighteen weeks. He was so covered with pus they could not touch him. They used to roll him from sheet to sheet, and soaked the sheets in vinegar afterwards, to disinfect them. His face became deeply pockmarked and for a long time he could not walk.

Ezekiel planned to go to America. Many Jews were going, but his wife would not hear of it. Her father said it might be better for them to move back to Elizavetgrad, and they did. Sarah Yetta was twelve and a half years old then. In a little while she began to sew for several families. As for her brothers— Michael worked in a lumberyard and Israel in a leather store;

Mordecai, Abram, and Rachmiel went to school; Fishel was still sick, and the doctors could do little for him. Whenever Ezekiel would say "America," Hannah would answer, "With a cripple?"

The Volskys lived in the suburbs behind the blacksmiths' street, near the fairgrounds. Their house was one of a row built almost underground: the roofs were only two feet above the street. The light came through four little windows. They had three rooms; one they used for a store-room and to work in. Hannah helped her stepmother at her stand in the market. Ezekiel did a little glazing; he tried many things.

One day Ezekiel came with a wagon. The driver carried chalk and cans of oil into the house. Ezekiel paid him fifteen copecks. "Only fifteen copecks for all that load?" Sarah Yetta asked.

"It is almost three o'clock," her father said, "and that is all he has earned today. How hard it is to make a living!"

"What new trade have you now?" she asked.

Her father sighed. "A store wants me to make putty. They pay fifteen copecks for forty pounds."

He mixed the chalk and oil and beat the mixture with a mallet. He began to sweat and often stopped to catch his breath. "I know an easier way than that," Sarah Yetta said, and took off her shoes and stockings. She danced on the putty until it was soft.

Now she had not only dough to knead for her mother but putty to make for her father. She became strong and wiry. But she used to wonder what would become of her. It seemed to her that she was just wasting her life in a hole in the ground. And when Saturday came, she could not read because her mother's stepmother would nag her; she was making her bad eyes worse and would soon be blind.

One day they caught a rat in a trap at the store of the merchant to whom Israel was apprenticed, and Israel's master told him to kill it; but Israel could not bring himself to do it. His master stamped on Israel's foot to make him kill the rat until his foot was so swollen he could hardly walk. He limped home, and Sarah Yetta bathed his foot and put medicine on it. When their father came, he sent Israel back to work. For some time he had to go about in a shoe cut open at the top. That Saturday when Israel came home to dinner, his face had grown worn and dark. After he had gone, Hannah cried and said, "Such young children with such old faces."

But Ezekiel said, "It is better so: they will grow strong and hard."

Three years went by. And then one day Ezekiel told his family that a man who had been a chum of his at school had hired him to buy grain for a mill. He was to be paid thirty roubles a month. By this time, too, Israel's apprenticeship in the leather store was up. He had worked only for board and clothes; now he was to have sixty roubles a year and his board. Israel gave thirty roubles to his father and the rest he kept for clothes.

Ezekiel bought a stout cloth, called "devil's cloth," and Hannah and Sarah Yetta made suits for the children. Sarah Yetta made herself a skirt and blouse of a dark blue goods. The blouse had a little red collar. And they moved to the city. Ezekiel bought half a dozen chairs with cane seats. In the middle of their new living-room they had a big round table and in the corner a divan covered with cretonne; the windows had white curtains.

The well was two blocks away. Of course, no *mademoiselle* could carry water through the street. Ezekiel told Mordecai it was his duty to fill the water-barrel. But if Sarah Yetta made him go, he would drop pail and line into the well and fishing them out was a lot of trouble. They could not afford to buy water: they used eight pails a day and it cost a copeck and a half a pail. Israel was now a salesman; he no longer had chores to do for his master's wife and had his evenings off. He would come home and help Sarah Yetta bring all the water they needed. But when he could not come, she carried in the water herself after dark.

Ezekiel used to go away on buying trips. He would come home for Saturday and Sunday. On Saturday he would go to synagogue with his sons. Weekdays, Hannah would leave early in the morning to help her stepmother. At four o'clock she would be back. Sarah Yetta used to be up at dawn, send the children off to school, do the housework, and then she had time enough to do her sewing. Altogether, they had rather a pleasant time of it. To the right of them lived a gentile, Anastasia Vladimirovna. Her husband had been killed in the Turkish War. One of her sons was studying to be a priest, another was in a government bureau, and her daughter was a school teacher. Across the way lived another widow. She had two daughters. The unmarried daughter was bright and knew Hebrew, but was homely. She and Sarah Yetta became great friends and found much to talk about. Near them was a family, the Olanovs, who seemed to have nothing to do with their neighbors.

Sarah Yetta made friends with Anastasia Vladimirovna. She was a good woman, anxious to help everyone. Though her son was studying to be a priest, she liked Jews. She taught Sarah Yetta how to sew dresses.

Once Anastasia said to Sarah Yetta, "Mrs. Olanov's niece, Rebecca, was here a little while ago. I don't believe she has eaten anything today: her lips were dry, and her body shivered. Neither she nor her aunt will do anything for themselves: they cannot sew on a button. Rebecca wants to meet you and will be back in a few minutes."

When she came in, Sarah Yetta went with her to her aunt.

Mrs. Olanov was a young woman with two small children. Sarah Yetta could see that they were all hungry. She brought seventy-five copecks of her savings to Anastasia for the Olanovs. After that Sarah Yetta became friendly with them. Mr. Olanov was a tutor. He had been unable to find work in Elizavetgrad and had gone to a place in the country. It was hard to send money from there, and so his wife and children and her niece were starving when Sarah Yetta first met them.

Mr. Olanov came home for a few days, and one night they gave a party. Sarah Yetta danced in the quadrilles, but when the boys and girls began a kissing game, she went off to have tea with the Olanovs. He looked at her so pityingly that she could not help laughing and said, "What are you thinking of?"

"I have heard that you do not enjoy life. You take life too seriously."

"Isn't life serious?"

"A young girl should enjoy it as other young people do."

"I certainly do not enjoy life, but I do not mean by enjoyment what you mean. I am sorry not to have an education, but as for the work I do, that is necessary. I do not mind it. I must carry my share of the burdens of the family. If I had an education, I should not mind the work I do. Anastasia Vladimirovna is of a noble family and highly educated, yet when she has rough work to do, she does it. Some people carry their education about as if on a plate and are afraid to stoop."

Mr. Olanov said, "I suppose you have been reading *Der Yiddishe Moujik*." (That was a book urging the Jews to give up trading and to work like the peasants.)

"No," she said, "but I'd like to. Do you mean to say," Sarah Yetta went on, "that if the water-carrier does not come until eleven o'clock because his horse fell on the way, a woman should keep her children in bed, unwashed and without breakfast, and not bring water from the well because she is a lady?"

The others came over to listen. "Well," said one, "let's take a walk. Goodnight," he said, and put out his left hand to shake hands with Sarah Yetta.

"Why the left?" she asked.

"It's nearer my heart."

"I'd rather have the right," she said.

They were all embarrassed. When the guests had gone, she asked Mr. Olanov if she had been wrong in saying what she did.

"He did not mean anything by that," Mr. Olanov said, "but you insulted him. Some day he may insult you."

"I am not afraid of his insults, and I do not like him. He thinks all the girls are in love with him."

"Do you know him?"

"Yes. He is an empty-headed fellow. His mother sells hot water and his sister sews jackets for peasants. A few weeks ago I was at a Zionist meeting: *there* were young fellows to look at and to listen to."

One day, Mrs. Olanov told Sarah Yetta that her father had come and would like to see Sarah Yetta. "You know my grandchild Rebecca—" he said, "her father left her mother about three years ago, and nothing has been heard of him since. I am not rich, but I thought I would give Rebecca five hundred roubles as a dowry and marry her off. What do you think?"

"Would she be provided for? You may only have another burden on your hands."

"That is why I spoke to you," he answered, "can she do the sewing you do?"

"I have tried to teach her, but she hasn't the knack for it. I think she would do better as a midwife. They do very well. She has gone to the *gymnasium*. Give her the money to take the course. Then, maybe, she'll find somebody fit for her. She's only seventeen and very bright."

In a few months the Olanovs moved away. Later, Sarah

Yetta had a letter from Rebecca: she was studying to be a midwife. Before Passover, her father asked Sarah Yetta to leave her sewing: a man who sold milk planned to bake matzoh, but the man to take charge had left him. They went to Velvel's that evening. He was tall and blond. His wife, Tilly, was beautiful and kind; she had a lovely complexion and black hair and eyes.

The street they lived on was muddy and so was the floor of their living room. Some bread was on the table and many glasses. In the room where the matzoh were to be baked were three large boards on which to roll the dough and a stone on which to knead it. Sarah Yetta swept and cleaned the room, and then the flour was brought in.

In the living room were Velvel's sons. Nahum looked like his mother—he had black hair and shining black eyes and a handsome face. He was clever, too. For supper each had a slice of bread and a glass of milk. Nahum was talking to Ezekiel as the others ate, and when he went to pour himself a glass of milk, the pitcher was empty. He took down another from the shelf. This was brim-full and some of the milk spilled on his head. "God blesses others with oil," he said, "but us with milk."

Next morning Sarah Yetta came early. About twenty-five girls and women worked for them. The fellow kneading the dough kept talking away, making fun of the girls. An old woman, jerking her head at Sarah Yetta, asked him, "What is the matter with her? You left her out."

"'Don't touch me!'" he answered, "is written on her face." She blushed and made believe she didn't hear.

Sometimes he made fun of a girl until she cried. At last Sarah Yetta went up to him and said, "You know that these girls are not happy at having to work here. They are ready to cry at an unkind word. You are an intelligent man, why make a fool of yourself?" He was as quiet after that as if he were dumb. She was glad to have found a remedy for him.

Sarah Yetta had been afraid that she would be unable to manage so many. But she tried to be natural and not flustered. And everything went smoothly. Her father and she had time for long talks. Every evening Nahum helped them with the bookkeeping. He hardly ever spoke to Sarah Yetta, but once he lent her a book.

After the holidays they went back to their own work. Ezekiel went away on his buying trips, and Sarah Yetta did her sewing at home. Her eldest brother, Michael—he sold wood to Velvel—said with a grin, "Nahum will give you more books, if you want them." And then he whispered to their mother and laughed. She told him not to be a fool. Sarah Yetta sent his book back to Nahum and he lent her another. She wondered why he did not come to see her, if he was thinking of her.

One evening as Israel and Sarah Yetta were going to the well, he told her he was worth more than he was getting. "But in this city," he said, "there are only small merchants. They cannot afford to hire me. I'm going to the fair at Poltava. There I'll meet many in my line."

She thought that great. Israel was only sixteen and already he spoke like a merchant. When they came back, they told their mother and her stepmother of his plan. But they did not like it at all. "Why didn't you tell Papa?" Hannah said.

And her stepmother said, "In one place even a stone grows. You must stay in one place."

Israel answered, "Change your place, change your luck. I have no luck here, I must change my place."

So he left for Poltava. A week went by and they had not heard from him. Her mother said it was all Sarah Yetta's fault. He would never have thought of going away, if not for her. Another week went by and at last a letter came. In it was a little

picture of Israel in new clothes. He was going to work in Kremenchuk for a hundred and twenty roubles a year, board and
lodging, and was to have half his wages in advance to send
home. They were very happy that evening. And in a few weeks
he sent them sixty roubles' worth of buckwheat.

Sarah Yetta had much to do and wanted a sewing machine to
do it quickly and better. But her mother's stepmother said,
"What are you going to become? A manufacturer? Get married."

Her mother, too, said that she was going to be an old maid
and a rope about her mother's neck. And her father said, "The
idea is good, but you can't do anything now with everybody
against you."

She wrote Israel about it. By return mail he sent her ten
roubles and wrote their mother to let her buy the sewing
machine. Soon she had some girls working for her. Anastasia
Vladimirovna was a great help, but she was going to move
away. She urged her to learn cutting from the books of the
Glazhdinsky system of dressmaking; but Sarah Yetta did not
have the money for it.

Their mother's stepmother became sick, and the doctor said she
had not long to live. They wrote to Grandfather Benjamin Hirsh.
But when his wife became better, he went away again. And then
she died. Ezekiel, too, was not at home for the funeral.

Later, Grandfather Benjamin Hirsh wrote them that he was
coming to stay. Sarah Yetta was afraid of him, because he was
so pious and whatever he said went. But she got along with
him as well as with her father. Though he was of the same generation as Grandfather Fivel, Grandfather Benjamin Hirsh did
not believe that Jews should study only their own books.

One day he told Hannah and Sarah Yetta about a nephew of his in Romania. "One of my sisters—a widow—died," he said, "and left a son in my care. He was bright and a good student. When he was about eighteen, the police went from door to door in our town and asked us all to sign our names. When they came to the house where my nephew was, he jumped out of a window. Late at night, he came to my bed and said, 'Uncle, you must help me. I wrote a letter to the Czar. That is why they are asking everybody to sign their names.' I asked him what he wrote and how he came to do it. 'I cannot tell you,' he said, 'but I wrote what should not have been written.' I used to send sugar to other towns and had many barrels in my yard. I made holes in one, put him inside, and got him over the border with a shipment. It took him three days to get to Romania. Now he owns a leather factory, and I want Israel to go there. It is just the place for him."

Once when he was watching Sarah Yetta at her work, her grandfather said, "My sisters could sew very well, and yet when we became poor, they could do nothing with their sewing."

"How did you become poor?" she asked.

"My father was the richest man in the town," he said. "He owned most of it. We built a home for old people and kept up a kitchen for the poor. I was the only son, and neither I nor Father's five sons-in-law had to work. We studied the Talmud. I was married when I was eighteen; and when I was in the thirties and had four children, I was still at my books. There was much to study, and I liked it. One of my school friends had become a doctor. Another had married a Brodsky and gone into their sugar business. But I stayed at my books. And then one fine morning Czar Nicholas sent an order that all should leave the town within twenty-four hours, Jews and gentiles: the houses and grounds were given to soldiers. We took what money we had and went to the nearest town; all had to do something for a living. I wrote to my friend who had married a Brodsky, and he asked me to come to Kiev. There I went into the business of shipping sugar. I did well until the railways were built. My wife died, and I married again. I didn't like my second wife. We had no children. My children were all married, and I went back to my books and ended up a teacher. That is all there is to it."

A woman of her acquaintance, Malka Cohen, sent for Sarah Yetta. Malka's son was to be married, and would Sarah Yetta make his underwear? Malka was very friendly, but when they talked price, she would pay five copecks less a piece than anyone else and no more. No matter how much Sarah Yetta spoke, and though she showed her how long the work would take and what it would cost, Malka would not pay more and said, "Do you want to be a Fanny Huebsch all at once?" (Fanny Huebsch had more sewing to do than any other seamstress in town.)

Sarah Yetta needed the work and took it at Malka's price. And Malka promised to tell her son's fiancée about Sarah Yetta. It took her until four o'clock to cut the goods. She carried the bundle and came home, flushed and tired. Her grandfather met her at the door. "I thought you were a sensible girl," he said. "You could have hired a carriage for fifteen copecks and not have carried that heavy bundle. That isn't sensible." Sarah Yetta saw two strangers at the table. She put the bundle away and went to see what the girls who worked for her had done.

She suspected that the elder of the two men was a matchmaker. The younger was about eighteen, but he wore clothes as old-fashioned as her grandfather Fivel's. After the two left, the matchmaker—for so he was—came back and had a brief talk with Grandfather Benjamin Hirsh. Then Grandfather Benjamin Hirsh went into the kitchen.

"Whom do you expect her to marry?" Sarah Yetta could hear her mother say.

"Do you want her to marry an ignorant fellow," said Grandfather Benjamin Hirsh, "a man a century behind the times? I had a talk with him: he knows nothing of the Talmud. He is just a religious fanatic, an empty-headed fellow who dresses up like his grandfather. I want her to marry a man of today who understands the world."

Next morning, her grandfather sat near Sarah Yetta and at last said, "I want to have a talk with you about your way of working. Yesterday you carried home a bundle too heavy for you, you worked until late at night, and this morning you are up so early at work again."

"You see, Grandfather, the people here won't pay what they ought to. One must work hard to make anything at all. Yesterday, I brought four dozen men's linen underwear to sew for Malka Cohen. She pays only twenty copecks a piece. The thread alone costs me six copecks, and I must pay my installments on the sewing machine, and my girls must get something. I spent four hours yesterday cutting up the goods, and now I must bring it back. And some won't pay you right away, but you must go again and again. The people of this town think they will become rich by squeezing what they can out of those who work for them."

"But if you work so hard," her grandfather said, "in the end you will be sick and that won't pay at all."

Ezekiel was hurrying through his prayers, and Sarah Yetta could see by his face that he had something to tell her. He put aside his prayer-shawl and phylacteries, washed himself again, said grace, and began his breakfast. "My daughter," he said, "I am not pleased at the way you talk. You should not go about as if the world were doing you harm. You will not change the world that way and will only harm yourself.

"Last week you had much to say against Isaac: he ran away and left his family without means! Now it turns out that he didn't desert them at all. As soon as he was over the border, he sent his parents a telegram to care for his family until he establishes himself. He isn't as bad as you thought, is he? Now, Malka Cohen is not rich. Her husband makes a good living, that is all. Malka does her own marketing. Why should you be better than anybody else she buys from? Thrifty women do not care whether you make money or lose: what they buy they want as cheap as possible."

"Then they are wrong," Sarah Yetta said. "They should care for others besides themselves. All of us work hard. Mamma, you, Israel and I, even Frieda works, and we haven't five roubles to our name."

"I am worried about Michael," said Ezekiel, thoughtfully. "His employer complained to me about him. I am sure he will not keep him much longer. And why should he? There are plenty of better men without work. Can you blame his employer? Even you wouldn't keep the girl who couldn't make buttonholes. You told me how poor her family is, that they haven't enough to eat, and yet you couldn't keep her, because she couldn't do her work. Even you," her father repeated with a smile.

Ezekiel finished his breakfast and said, "Bad times, my daughter. You must be satisfied with things as they are. Work and be content."

Bad times! She thought of all the carriages on the boulevard and the ladies and gentlemen riding about in them, but she was afraid to say anything: she would be thought a nihilist.

* * *

That day Sarah Yetta was called to another kind of family than Malka's. Mr. Klarfeld dealt in sheep. His eldest son was studying medicine. She was met by the eldest daughter who was very friendly. In a little while Mrs. Klarfeld came in. Sarah Yetta showed her samples. "So young," Mrs. Klarfeld said, "and you do this work?"

"I have done it since I was twelve," she answered.

Mrs. Klarfeld gave her two rolls of linen and the pattern of her son's underwear. Sarah Yetta was to have it ready in two weeks. "Buy the buttons yourself and add it to the bill," Mrs. Klarfeld said. For the first time Sarah Yetta was in a house where every inch of goods was not measured and the price not haggled over. She was overjoyed at their friendliness and trust in her.

So, little by little, she built up a trade until she had four sewing machines and eight girls working for her. Among these, for a while, was her landlady's daughter. The landlady was a widow and could not make a living. She asked Sarah Yetta to teach her daughter to sew. The daughter worked hard, but could do nothing that called for intelligence: she could only run off straight seams on the machine. Sarah Yetta taught her to sew peasant blouses—these came ready-cut from the store— and took her to Hyamovsky. She made a sample, and he said he would give her blouses to sew. She and Sarah Yetta then went to the Singer Sewing Machine Company, and Sarah Yetta bought a machine for her. She paid them ten roubles and was to pay the rest, a rouble a week. In about three months the company sent Sarah Yetta twenty-five roubles. She asked her parents if she should give their landlady's daughter the commission. Ezekiel said, "Anastasia Vladimirovna made twenty-five roubles on your first machine. You have earned the money. Now you can buy the books from which to learn dressmaking—or a wardrobe in which to lock the goods at night. Then you needn't worry so about thieves." They decided that she ought to buy the wardrobe first, and Sarah Yetta bought one for eighteen roubles.

Michael was out of work and became a glazier. Mordecai worked in a clothing store on the main street. He came home every night for supper and afterwards went for a walk along the boulevard. One day Hannah received a letter; she could not read Russian and took the letter to have Mordecai read it—he was not in the store and had not been for three weeks. She almost fainted. She waited for him to come to supper. He came at the usual time, singing and jigging, jolly as always. Whenever he was home, the house was full of laughter. After supper, he took his cane to go out. Hannah stopped him. At her grave face, he smiled and said, "Now it is coming."

"What do you mean?" his mother said. "What do you do?"

"I did something just as an experiment. If it turned out well, I was going to tell you about it. I want to learn how to make clothes instead of selling them. I don't like to sell. It's no crime to be a workingman."

"I don't understand you," said his mother. "What are you doing?"

"I've apprenticed myself to a tailor."

"Why didn't you ask us first? Perhaps we don't want you to be a tailor."

"I know you don't. That's why I didn't ask."

"I don't mind the kind of work but the people with whom you'll have to work."

"I'm working for a fine man," and he told her his name. His mother agreed that he had a good reputation. "And," Mordecai added, "he is a military tailor. I am learning how to make clothes for officers."

"The rakes! The good-for-nothings!" his mother said. "It will not be much to your credit to mix with such people."

"Well," said Mordecai, "if you want to be good, you can be, no matter with whom you are." At this, Grandfather Benjamin Hirsh came in and Hannah said no more, to spare him the news. But he saw that she and Sarah Yetta were troubled. Mordecai went for his walk, and her father asked Hannah what worried her.

"We kept Mordecai at home until he was fourteen," she said, "and gave him an education we did not give Michael or Israel, only to have him disgrace us by apprenticing himself to a tailor."

But her father took the news calmly. "You can't choose for your children," he said. "They have their own likes and dislikes. It is better for them to be free from their mother's apron strings. He is old enough to know what he is doing."

"We thought him the cleverest of all," said Hannah, "and he turns out to be so unambitious—so low."

"A trade is not low," said her father angrily. "What happened to your brother Solomon should have taught you not to make children do what they don't want to. Be content to let them go their own way as long as it is honorable." And her grandfather turned to Sarah Yetta, "I brought up my three sons to be rabbis. Solomon was only seventeen when he finished his studies. The next year he married the daughter of a rabbi, and became a rabbi in a small town. He had also to kill the animals used for food. This upset him and he wanted to give up his position. He was making a good living, and his wife and I made him stay at it. And what happened? One day, without a word to either of us, he gave it up and from that time on spoke to no one. Well, his wife and children had to go to her family, and he wandered about from town to town. At last he settled down in a village as a teacher of little children."

Hannah sighed, "Oh, what luck I have!"

When Ezekiel came home in a few weeks, he had a talk with Mordecai. His father wanted to see his employer. But Mordecai

said, "I'm working for this man just on trial. He's a master crafts-
man. You know boys are apprenticed to tailors for three years
before they learn anything worthwhile. But I can sew now parts
of a coat as well as anybody. And I don't have to do any work
about the house. That was made up between us. I won't mind
the children or bring water. As soon as I finish work in the shop
and have my supper, I am free. If you interfere and make me
leave, you'll be blamed, just as you were blamed when I left
the store. I am fifteen now and can fight my own battles."

"Have it your way," said his father, "but I hope you'll be an
honest fellow."

Saturdays Mordecai visited his father and mother. He was
happy and looked well, so they were satisfied. One evening it
was chilly, and Hannah had the door closed. A woman banged
it open, her eyes blazing. Hannah recognized her. She sold
chickens in the market. Without greeting Hannah, "Where's
Mordecai?" she shouted.

Hannah trembled. "What do you want with Mordecai?"

Her visitor said sarcastically, "Look at the woman! Just see
how she knows of nothing!"

Hannah said quietly, "But what do you want?"

The woman began to scream at the top of her voice. When
she quieted down, Hannah insisted that she tell her what had
happened. "I set the table," she said, "and while I made supper
for him, I sent Mordecai for water to make him tea. I waited
and waited and waited and no Mordecai. At last I went outside
to look for him, and there was the kettle thrown into a corner.
Where's Mordecai?"

"Shout and scream as much as you like and have all the
neighbors in," Hannah said, "but I can't tell you where he is,
because he didn't come home."

Saturday Mordecai came as usual and his mother said, "It

wouldn't have hurt you any to have gone for water for your
own tea."

Mordecai smiled. "I'm fifteen," he said. "I'm a man and I
won't bring water if it's only from across the street. She won't
work me as she does the other apprentices. And I was not supposed to help her. This was made up between my master and
me. He doesn't keep his word. He promised me ten roubles for
a pair of shoes two weeks ago. I was going about barefoot, and
still he didn't give me the money. So I found another place
and am working there now."

"I wish you could eat and sleep at home," Hannah said, "no
matter how little you'll be paid. What a family you worked for!
Even if this is a better one, it could not be much better."

"I don't like to eat where I work," said Mordecai, "and the
first chance I get, I'll eat and sleep at home."

"But you must keep your word, my son, or you'll have a
bad name."

Mordecai smiled. "Oh, I am reasonable."

It was not long before he had his meals at home. His little
sister Frieda had to have pot roast ready for him every evening.
Sometimes, when the wood was damp and the potatoes would
not brown just right, her black eyes would fill with tears at the
thought that Mordecai might not like his supper. And then he
would not eat at home, and Mother wanted him to. But Mordecai never asked what they had to eat.

When Grandfather Benjamin Hirsh was seventy-three years
old, he went to visit all his children. He left in the spring and
came back late in autumn. Then he told Hannah how poor
some of her brothers and sisters were and the children of those
better off were not as he wished. He spoke much of his nephew

in Romania. He wanted Israel to go there and escape service in the army. But Ezekiel would say, "Why go from one bad country to another? It is better to go to America."

And Hannah said, "Israel's time to serve is still many years off. Who knows what will happen until then?"

"Yes, yes," said her father, "but you don't know how quickly that time will come."

One very hot day in July, he was too sick to go to synagogue and prayed at home. He became worse, and Sarah Yetta called the doctor. After he was gone, her grandfather smiled and said, "What did the doctor prescribe?"

"A physic."

"I thought so."

"Why, Grandfather, don't you believe in doctors?"

"Not when they can't help you. I know that I am old, and my strength is going." Sarah Yetta was sick at heart. She kept thinking, A man like that dies, and there is no one in the family to take his place.

Grandfather Benjamin Hirsh wrote letters to his friends and had Ezekiel call the head of the burial committee. Benjamin Hirsh told him where he wished to be buried, and they agreed upon the cost of the funeral. Then Benjamin Hirsh called Ezekiel to his bedside and said, "The day I close my eyes you must take my fur hat, my new clothes, and what is left of my money and send it to Moses, my youngest son. He is worse off than the rest of you." The next day he died.

That winter was a hard one. It was hard enough to make a living, and on top of that, they were afraid of a pogrom. In the spring, somehow, they became hopeful of better times, though for no better reason, perhaps, than the sunny weather.

One dawn, as Ezekiel was saying his prayers and the children were dressing, the man who sold him lottery tickets came in. "At last I have good news for you," he said, "your number won, Mr. Volsky."

Ezekiel asked to see the bulletin to make sure and saw that number thirty-one had won. He had thirty. He sighed and said, "How the money would have helped us."

The man looked through his notes. "Gedaliah, Velvel the milkman's son, won," he said. At this Ezekiel looked at Sarah Yetta. She was blushing. Velvel's son, Nahum, wished to marry her. He had said so to her father. But Nahum was soon to go away for his army service, and so Ezekiel did not think the match advisable. Though she kept telling herself nothing would come of it, whenever Sarah Yetta thought of Nahum, she said to herself, maybe. But now she was sure he would not have her. His brother would give him some of his money, and he would not have to marry a penniless girl.

In the autumn Nahum was taken to the army. He said good-by to her father and brothers, but did not come to see Sarah Yetta. That evening she heard her father say to her mother, "His going away is worse than that of a son. A son will come back some time. Nahum has five years to serve and it will be hard to get another man like that for our daughter."

Next year Michael went to serve his term in the army, but he was let off because he was the eldest son. His father had to go to army headquarters with some papers for Michael. A newly drafted soldier, still drunk, hit Ezekiel in the side. He was not strong, and the blow weakened him greatly. It pained him all year.

One day, Sarah Yetta happened to go to a house near the market for some work, but the woman was out. It was late in the afternoon. Her mother always had a good many parcels to

carry home, and she thought she would help her. But as Sarah
Yetta came near the stand, she saw her mother coming along
with a young man.

"Do you recognize him?" Hannah asked. "This is Saul Rubinov, Simon's son."

"How could I recognize him? I haven't seen him since we
moved from Snamenka."

Saul Rubinov had come to stay a while in Elizavetgrad. Sarah
Yetta was two years older than he and considered herself an
elder sister. They spoke of many things, agreed and disagreed
and quarrelled. She introduced him to her friends. "What
homely girls you go with," he said.

"I am not better looking."

"Oh, yes you are. Your forehead and eyebrows are beautiful, and your figure is better than theirs." She thought, Nahum
liked my long hair, he likes my forehead and eyebrows and figure; perhaps, I am not so bad-looking. Her little sister Frieda
came over, and Sarah Yetta said, "Here is what I call a good-
looking girl." Frieda had beautiful lips and eyes and an olive
complexion.

"But you are cleverer," Saul said. "I remember you at her
age. You were a terror. You bossed the whole house."

"I still boss my brothers. But there's one I can't do anything
with. That's Mordecai."

"He's too smart for you."

"But," Sarah Yetta answered, "everyone ought to do his
share of the work. He isn't smart, but unfair. And Mordecai
just did a most unpleasant thing. He apprenticed himself to a
tailor."

"Why is that so unpleasant? It's an honest trade."

"Yes, tailoring is honest, but tailors are not. If Mordecai
wants to be a tailor, don't let him say he became one because
it's an honest trade." Then they spoke of Israel. The more she

praised him, the angrier Saul became. At last he called her a liar. He was her parents' guest, and so she said nothing. When his visit was over, they agreed that he was clever, but rather outspoken.

A few weeks later his mother came to their house. She had a bad headache, but in the morning she was better and called to Sarah Yetta's father in the tone of a rich lady, "I want a few words with you, Ezekiel." He was in a hurry to go to business, but, of course, he had to listen. "Last night my head hurt so I could not talk to you." And Sarah Yetta heard no more of what she said.

But at last Ezekiel answered, "Your son is bright, but he is too young and still has his term in the army to serve. You can't be as old-fashioned as your father! He married you off at fifteen without asking you for your consent, and you know how you suffered. And now you want to do the same to your son. And my daughter is two years older than Saul. It would be ridiculous for them to marry. I know it is written that at eighteen a man should marry; but it is also written, Build a house and plant a vineyard, then marry."

Ezekiel's family became very friendly with the Rubinovs. Elizavetgrad was the nearest city to their village, and Saul, his father and mother, his brothers and sisters, would often come to town. When Saul's father, Simon, came, Ezekiel and Simon Rubinov sat up until late at night in talk.

In September, Ezekiel told his family that he was going away on a trip that would take a long time. He was to be paid thirty roubles a month besides his expenses. "Now," he said to Sarah Yetta, "you will be able to keep most of your money for yourself, and I hope you'll have enough for the course you want to buy." He planned to see his son Israel, too.

It wasn't long before Sarah Yetta sent for Glazhdinsky's *System of Cutting for Dressmakers and Tailors.* The books and an instructor's lessons cost fifty roubles. But she was soon able to make dresses that fit. She also copied the patterns in any size for tailors and was paid fifty copecks each. This was easy money and cost her nothing but time, for the tailors furnished the paper. Here, it seemed to her, was a good business for her father, and she was eager to have him home: he was quick and would have no trouble making the patterns. She now made house-dresses, too. This was much better than sewing linen. She was paid a rouble and a half for the cheapest dress, and all it cost her was two copecks for thread. (She was paid twenty copecks for a shirt and the thread cost her six.) Things were beginning to look brighter.

Ezekiel had been away two months. Now the weather be-came bad—heavy rains and deep slush in the streets. Some days people could not leave their homes. And there were many sud-den deaths. Soon all knew that there was an epidemic in the country: influenza. Ezekiel sent many letters home and at last one that made them uneasy. As they read it, they felt that he was unwell, but they did not speak of their fear.

One night Sarah Yetta went to sleep late, tired and worried. She dreamt that she was in their yard. There was a fiery cloud in the sky, and as she looked at it, it seemed like a lion. She went into the house, and there she found a woman who had lived near them in Dmitrovka. I know I am dreaming, Sarah Yetta said, but I just saw a burning-red lion in the sky. That is a sign that your father is dead, the woman answered. Sarah Yetta screamed and woke, relieved to find it was all a dream.

For a long time she could not fall asleep, and then she dreamt again. She was cutting black goods into a dress and someone asked her what she was doing that for. Why, I have to wear it, she answered. She woke up and found her mother beside her. "What is the matter with you?" Hannah asked. Sarah Yetta's cheeks were wet with tears, and she shook for cold.

She dressed herself and tried to forget her dreams. Her mother said, "I suppose you were reading a silly novel before you went to bed." Sarah Yetta told her nothing and went for a long walk. It was Saturday. When she came back, Sarah Yetta prayed with all her might, chanted psalms, and wept bitterly, taking care that her mother should not see her. She felt a little better after that. They all had dinner; the younger children were joking, and Mordecai danced about and played with them: it was very lively.

In three weeks they had a letter from Ezekiel that he was on his way home. This was on a Monday. Wednesday they had another letter that he was sick, and he wrote that as soon as he reached his stopping-place he would send them his address. On the very next day they had a telegram from a hospital in Ekaterinoslav: Ezekiel had been taken there. Michael left on the next train.

When the telegram came, Sarah Yetta did not talk, she could not cry or pray. She just waited. She thought, How can Michael bring Father home when he is sick? And in this weather? And then she was afraid to think. She began to watch the door Friday morning, though she knew Michael could not possibly come before six at night. She waited until it was dark. The table was set, the five candles lit, and they had their supper. Someone said, "Religious people ought not to cry on Saturday," and Sarah Yetta began to cry. She could not stop. She sat at the window and watched the yard. At nine o'clock a messenger came in. She sprang to the door and tore open the telegram. It was from Michael; the message had only two words: *he died.*

When she came to, her arm hurt her: she had fallen on it. Mordecai had just come in; he still had his coat on. He was saying, "What are you screaming for, you crazy girl?"

"Father's dead!"

"Well, he's dead and buried, and you can't help him now."

"Oh, how can you be so cold?"

"I found Rachmiel outside in his shirt screaming away like you."

"But how did you find out?"

"The messenger met me, so I hurried home."

Sarah Yetta saw nothing and thought of nothing, she only wailed. Late at night, her mother came to quiet her and took her in her arms. They wept together a long time. When Sarah Yetta opened her eyes Saturday morning her mother was reading the prayers. Somebody told Sarah Yetta that on Saturday mourners must not cry, because the day is a festival. But how could she help it? In the evening about ten men came and made the prescribed cuts in their clothing; and her brothers said the prayer for the dead.

The first three days of mourning, the neighbors prepared their meals. Their mother, Sarah Yetta, Mordecai, and Abram sat on the floor, as the custom is; but Frieda was only eleven and did not have to, nor Rachmiel, who was nine. Fishel was not quite seven. Since Hannah was in business, she was told she might go to her stand even on the third day, but she felt that she could not.

On Wednesday they found Rachmiel sick. He had a headache and a pain in his side. Sarah Yetta and her mother took towels, wet them in cold water, and put them to his head and body.

They hardly knew what they were doing. But on Friday, their mother stood up from the floor, and told them all to stand up. She was always so quiet that they were not prepared to hear her say, "We must all be heroes now and not cry or complain. We must carry the burden Father carried, until the younger children can help themselves."

Monday, Hannah went to business. Sarah Yetta was about to begin her work, but she saw that Rachmiel was weak and pale. She carried him to the doctor. When she came in, the doctor asked, "What happened to you? Were you sick?"

"No," she said, "but my father died."

Dr. Rosenstein shook his head. "A young man, a young man. When I came to Elizavetgrad to study, he was eighteen years old. He used to bring sweet biscuits to those of us too poor to go home holidays. He was well off then.... How times flies."

"Yes," Sarah Yetta said, "he was eighteen then, and I am twenty now."

"What did he die of?"

"Pneumonia."

He examined her brother. "What did you do to him?" She told him. "Well, he had pneumonia, too, but he is getting better now."

On the way home, Rachmiel fell asleep. Sarah Yetta thought that he was dying. She had ten more blocks to go and reached home in a sweat. But a neighbor reassured her. "He is only asleep," she said. "Don't wake him. Sleep is better than medicine."

Michael had written that it had taken him more than twenty-four hours from Elizavetgrad to Ekaterinoslav, and when he came there, he found his father buried.

On his way back, Michael was going to stop at a number of towns to try to earn his fare.

He brought Ezekiel's baggage. Hannah opened it, and on top she found a bundle of long sheets of paper, carefully wrapped. They were covered with verse in Hebrew, and Abram was the only one of them who could read it at all. Ezekiel had been somewhat free in his speech, and Hannah was afraid there might be something nihilistic in his writing that would get them all into trouble. She was afraid to ask an outsider what the writing was about. In those days it was enough to say of a family, "They are nihilists," to have them arrested at once; the police investigated at their leisure. There was too much to burn at one time, so she burnt a few sheets every morning until all were gone. As she put the first into the fire she said, "Here's a man's life."

They had to give up one of their three rooms to make ends meet. Hannah brought a woman to look at the room, and as she saw them coming into the yard, dressed in black and in heavy boots, Sarah Yetta said to herself, "The same uniform: they are from the same club." Malka liked the room, and she said to Sarah Yetta, "I have a little daughter, Duba, eleven years old. You'll take her among your girls and teach her to sew, won't you?" Malka's husband had been a capmaker. He was taken sick with influenza at a fair and died there. She had two children: her elder daughter was engaged to a capmaker, and only Duba was on her hands.

One of Ezekiel's acquaintances called on Hannah. He would put Israel in business for himself, if Israel would go into partnership with his son, Benjamin. When Saul Rubinov's mother came to town, they told her what was being planned for Israel. She said that she would furnish the money if Israel and Saul became partners. The Volskys knew Benjamin to be a wild fellow. It seemed to them that Saul would make a better partner, though the Rubinovs were not as rich as Benjamin's father. Sarah Yetta wrote Israel of both offers. He answered that on his way home he would stop at Snamenka and see the Rubinovs; but that was nine months off: he would not be free until then.

The president of the city school was another acquaintance of Ezekiel's. (They had been at school together.) He had no children. He asked Hannah to come to his house, and when she did, offered to adopt Rachmiel. She thought this excellent for Rachmiel, but he asked, "What will I have to do?"

"You'll be his son. You'll have a good education, go to the *gymnasium* and the university. You'll have the best of everything, but you'll have to call him father and have his name."

Rachmiel—he was only nine—said, "I certainly should like to be a learned man, but I won't take his name and call him father instead of my father. I'll go to work as Israel and Abram did, and be a self-made man." In the spring, Abram told them that Tsali Kaminski wanted an errand boy, and Rachmiel would do. The Volskys were supposed to clothe and feed him. But in a week, dressed in a new white suit, he brought his other clothes home, and told them Mrs. Kaminski would give him clothes and food and had even promised him some education.

When Ezekiel had been dead for a year, the eldest son of Moses Spectorov—the man who had swindled Grandfather Fivel out of his house—came to ask Fivel's forgiveness. Moses Spectorov was dead and his son, the lawyer, had died of consumption when still young. Spectorov's eldest son had just lost his own son. Though he was not rich he wanted to pay Fivel something for the house. Grandfather Fivel would not take it. "Not now, not now," he said. "God will judge between us."

A brother-in-law of one of Hannah's neighbors and his son, Isaac, came to the fair in the city. They were from a village near Poland and spoke a Yiddish unlike that of Elizavetgrad. When the fair was over, the neighbor asked Sarah Yetta if she liked Isaac. "Oh," Sarah Yetta said, not thinking of anything, "he's nice enough for a country boy."

The neighbor said, "He's young, he's only twenty-one, but he's the eldest and doesn't have to serve in the army. He likes you, and if you want me to, I'll write him, and he'll be back in a few weeks, and you'll be engaged."

Sarah Yetta was surprised and told her that she would let her know. She wanted to think it over. She was sure that she could not have Nahum. He had still three years to serve, and his family had become rich, and the Volskys were poorer than ever. Her neighbor's nephew was not bad-looking and not a fool. If he would live in the city and be among merchants instead of peasants, Sarah Yetta thought, he would be no worse than her brothers.

When Isaac came, Sarah Yetta told him that if they were to marry, they must live in the city. She did not want any jewelry or fine clothes, she was willing to keep on as she had been doing—she had four machines now—she would help him all she could, but she would not go into the country to live, even if she would only have a piece of bread every other day in the city. "It's so stupid in the country. I had a taste of it for several years. If your family will say yes to your living in the city, we may become engaged."

During the summer they wrote to each other. In the autumn, Isaac and his father came again to the fair. They brought Sarah Yetta two rings and a pair of earrings and wanted to have the formal engagement at Christmas.

Israel was coming home. With him came Simon Rubinov and his son Saul. They had agreed upon a partnership and were to open a leather store; Saul was to stay with the Volskys.

Saul Rubinov was always finding fault with Sarah Yetta. He would call her proud. She would say that she could not be proud, because she knew so little and was not as beautiful or as wise as she would like to be.

Malka, the widow who lived with the Volskys, stood in the doorway of her room and said, "He is right: you are proud."

"But why do you think so?"

"You never go out with the other girls. You think yourself better than they."

Sarah Yetta explained that the girls wanted to walk on the boulevard Saturday afternoon, but that she walked about all week and wanted to rest Saturday. "And I don't get a chance to read all week, but Saturday is my day for reading."

"What you say shows that you think yourself better than they!" cried Malka.

Saul found out that Sarah Yetta was to be engaged. His mother came to see Hannah and objected. At Christmas time, Isaac's mother came and tried to persuade Sarah Yetta to live in the country. "You'll get married," she said, "and you'll open a little store and you'll live there. You can do better there than here with your sewing machines."

There were other guests and they talked about life in a village. "Isaac ought to live in the city among merchants," Sarah Yetta said. "And, besides, once you are settled in the country, it is very hard to bring up children properly, because there are no schools."

Isaac's mother said, "She is already thinking about educating her children." Sarah Yetta blushed, and everybody laughed.

When she picked up courage to speak again, she said, "The door is wide open when you go in; but it is very narrow when you want to come out. I'll go to any city or even to America, but I'll never go into the country."

The guests became angry at her. One said, "What is she dreaming of?" And another, "She wants to fly high."

She answered, "I cannot help it, I was born that way."

Next morning Isaac came to talk to her. They were alone. "You ought to give in to my mother now," he said, "and when we are married, we'll have our own way."

"I don't want to fool anybody, Isaac. And I won't break your mother's heart. I won't even visit you there. I hate the country."

"You didn't have to say you want to go to America."

"But I do want to go."

"Well, Mother said that she didn't want us to become engaged, because it would not be right for us to break it off afterwards, since you have no father."

As he was saying this, Sarah Yetta took off his rings and earrings. She went to her chest of drawers and took out the little box lined with red velvet in which they had come. She put them neatly inside. Isaac was still talking and did not notice what she was doing.

"Here are your presents, Isaac," she said. "I am the one to break our engagement. Good luck to both of us, and you go your way and I'll go mine."

He turned pale. She thought he was going to faint. He didn't touch the box, but stood up and went out. Sarah Yetta sent her little sister with the presents to his aunt's house.

What a lot of talk about it followed! Her family, too, were against Sarah Yetta. "Why am I wrong?" she asked. "If he will live in the city, I will not break the engagement. I told him all that before we became engaged."

Her mother and brothers said, "It doesn't matter where you live: you can be happy anywhere." Finally, her brother Israel and Saul Rubinov went to see the place where Isaac lived. When they came back, Israel did not say a word, but Saul had a great deal to say. He said that she would not be able to stand it one day. "Why, Snamenka," he said, "is a place of refinement compared to that village. The peasantry there is worse than ours, and there is no other Jewish family."

Hannah shook her head. "I hope you won't feel sorry."

"Mamma," Sarah Yetta said, "let me go to America."

"You inherited that idea from your father."

"I don't see why we are staying here. Many people have gone to America, and they are better off."

"Maybe if they were here, they'd be better off too, and if we were there, we'd be badly off. God is everywhere."

"But doesn't the Talmud say, 'Change your place, change your luck'?"

"You're too smart, my daughter," she said and went out of the room.

Many matchmakers came, and Sarah Yetta had other suitors. Her father had said, "If you want to make a good match, marry somebody twenty percent beneath you"; but these, she thought, were one hundred percent beneath her.

So a year and a half went by. Israel had to serve his term in the army. The Volskys never thought he would have to go, because he was short-winded; but he was the first of the Jewish quota to be taken. Now they could not see how they would keep up the family. In a few weeks Israel's business would have to be sold: Saul did not want to stay. Though he was the eldest son, in another year he would have to serve, too.

"Israel," Sarah Yetta said, "let us both go to America. We'll do well there, and then we can bring the others over. We have enough money just now to go."

He became angry and looked at her with his large black eyes: "I am ashamed of you when I hear you talk that way. Why should you want to go to America? Who goes there but bankrupts, embezzlers, and those who have wrecked their lives here?"

"Every intelligent person who can see farther than he can see from his window goes there now."

"Well," he answered, "then I am not intelligent enough."

Sarah Yetta showed him how bad things would be with them if he had to serve four years. "But I expect to be out in nine months," he said.

"I hope so, too," she said, "but I had also hoped that you would not have to serve at all."

Israel went away at Christmas. Before he left, Sarah Yetta

asked him to take a trip to their uncle Abram Loeb to see Grand-father Fivel.

"I hope I don't have to go to him soon," said Israel.

"Why not?"

"He is dead."

"Why didn't you tell me?"

"We had the other grandchildren there, but you were so upset over Father's death, we were afraid to tell you."

That winter was a hard one. The slush in the streets was so deep they could hardly go from house to house.

One Saturday night, Hannah had just lit the lamp, and Sarah Yetta was arranging her work for the next day, when in came Arele, the cantor. He said, "Good evening," and then looked at Sarah Yetta. He made a wry face. "So, this is your daughter," he said to Hannah. "Pst, what a beauty! And all the money she has!" He took a pinch of snuff. "Why does she make such a fuss? Much nicer girls than she haven't a chance now."

"Why do you insult me?" Sarah Yetta said. "That's a nice way to begin the week."

"I have a right to insult you. I was your father's friend."

"Oh, my father had a lot of good friends."

"But," said Arele, "be reasonable. There's a young man who wants you. His mother is willing to give away her house and everything she has. He's good-looking, too." And he told them his name.

"Oh, yes," Sarah Yetta said, "he's very good-looking, prettier than any girl I know. I have nothing against him, but I don't like him."

"What do you mean *like him?* You'll learn to like him when you're married."

Hannah said bitterly, "Really, they are honest, decent people."

"Well," said Arele, "I'm going to make an appointment for tomorrow at three o'clock. You'll see him again, and you'll like him." Sarah Yetta said nothing. "He'll be here with his mother. Goodnight."

When he was gone, Hannah said, "What objection have you to this young man?"

"He stutters so. He makes me sick when he talks."

The next day at three o'clock they came. They had tea. Hannah and his mother talked. Sarah Yetta said little. His mother had heavy old-fashioned jewelry on and she said, "I'll give you all, all, if you'll be a good daughter to me."

"I don't wear any jewelry," Sarah Yetta said.

"Oh, everybody wears jewelry. You must wear it too."

And they went away. The engagement was to take place next day at four o'clock. They had not asked Sarah Yetta; her mother had said yes, and Sarah Yetta did not know what to say. She did not want to hurt her mother—she was so set on marrying her off.

Next day, as always, Hannah went away at dawn. Sarah Yetta rose a little later: she used to go to bed late. At seven o'clock the girls who worked for her came. She did not know what to do. She did not want to become engaged to this fellow, because she did not want to marry him. Everybody knew that she had broken one engagement and to break another would be dreadful. At two o'clock she went off to see her customers and did not come back until ten at night. Her mother was waiting for her. "What have you done?" Hannah said. "Why didn't you tell me last night you didn't want the match?" They argued and argued and in the end both cried.

The day after Easter, Sarah Yetta heard shouts and cheers outside. She ran into the yard and met their landlady and her daughter at the gate. Many men were running along the street. Sarah Yetta had never seen any of them before.

"What is it?" she asked the landlady. "A fire?"

"No," she said, "they are going to kill the *sheenies*."

"Oh," Sarah Yetta said, "and you whose daughter I taught how to sew say this, you who are always telling me how much I did for you!"

"I can't help it," she answered, "but they are going to beat them up."

It was an hour and a half before all the Volskys were home. Her brothers locked the shutters and windows and barred the doors. "Wouldn't it have been better to have gone to America when Father wanted us to?" Sarah Yetta said. "Now we have nowhere to hide."

"God is everywhere," her mother answered.

The riot was over in another hour, but the depression lasted. Many Jews were going to America as soon as they could. Nobody felt like doing business.

In about a week, Abram Loeb, Ezekiel's brother, came to Elizavetgrad. "You did a dreadful thing," he said to Sarah Yetta. "Arele told me about it. How can you face anyone? It is true that you are not ugly, but if you've outrun the homely girls, you've not overtaken the pretty ones. And, besides, you're so poor."

"Uncle, why should I marry someone I don't care for? That would not be honest."

"I know you," he said, "you'll make a good wife. Do you expect to be in love?"

"No, but I want to respect the man I marry. I could not respect that fellow.... Uncle, I want to go to America, but I have no money now. I have only fifty roubles in the bank and less every day."

Abram Loeb thought a while. "I'll give you fifty roubles to help you to America," he said, "but you must keep it a secret. Even when you are in America, you must tell nobody. I have many relatives, and I can't help everyone."

The thought of America was balm to her. She felt stronger than ever.

Michael, her eldest brother, could find no work. Their mother had a sister in a small town near a brewery. Her son met Michael at the fair in Elizavetgrad and told Michael he would try to have him hired as a glazier in the brewery. In a few weeks he wrote Michael that he had work for him. Sarah Yetta lent him money for the fare. In a week Michael was back and told her he was engaged to their aunt's eldest daughter.

"But how can you get married," Sarah Yetta said, "if you can't even make a living for yourself? And why didn't you stay there?"

"Ah, sister," he said, "it's worse there than here."

"Then how are you going to get married?"

"They promised her a little store, and I'll do what I am doing now."

"But you are not doing anything now."

"I didn't want to be engaged to her. They wanted me to be engaged. They told me there was going to be an engagement that day and when I came, I found that I was the one to be engaged. And I couldn't say no before all the guests and put her to shame. I don't know what is going to come of it," and the tears rolled down his cheeks.

In a few weeks the girl came to see the Volskys. Sarah Yetta didn't like her at all, but Hannah told Sarah Yetta not to say a word.

Her brother married and was worse off than ever. He could not live with his wife's people: they had nine children and were glad to be rid of one. So Michael and his wife lived with his mother.

Israel had served nine months in the army, but he was not let off and still had three years and three months to serve. He became sick. In the hospital he tore out the fly-leaf of a book and wrote Sarah Yetta, "My dear sister, go to America. It is God's will." Her mother, too, at last consented. "You want to go and you'll have to go, I suppose."

"I don't want to go, if you don't want me to. You must want it with all your heart, or I won't go."

"How can I want it?" Hannah said. "You know how I'll miss you."

"What would you do if I were married and had to go to some village where you would not see me for years? You would want that, but you do not want me to go where it will be good for us."

"How do you know it will be?"

Elka Budinov, who lived across the street, was going to America in three weeks. Her husband had been there nine months and had sent her steamship tickets and money for herself and the children. Sarah Yetta was eager to go with her.

On the fast of the ninth of Ab, Sarah Yetta fasted too, and went to the cemetery. On the way she met Saul Rubinov coming to the city in a wagon. He jumped down. "What are you doing here?" he asked. She had not seen him since Israel went away. She told him that she was going to pray at the graves of her family before she went to America. She told him, too, how sorry she was not to be able to go to her father's grave, but she could not afford the fare.

"So you are going to America," he said.

"Yes, that is the only way to better ourselves."

"Well," he said, "I'll tell you a secret: I'm going to America too. I'm now on my way to Elizavetgrad to arrange to go with the Budinovs."

"And your parents let you go?"

"Oh, my mother has changed a good deal since your brother had to serve."

Three weeks went by. Mrs. Budinov left for America. And then one day Hannah came home at one o'clock instead of four. She put her basket down and wiped the sweat from her face.

"What have you there, Mamma?" Sarah Yetta asked. "Are you going to make me an engagement party?"

"I suppose I am not worthy of that. I met Nahum Levitsky. They are going to America in two weeks and will take you along. I'm going to make you zwieback for the trip. Finish your work and sell out whatever you have and God take care of you."

Sarah Yetta was worried about her sister Frieda and youngest brother Fishel. Frieda was almost fourteen. Where could she find work when Sarah Yetta was gone? Fishel was weak and not bright and had not learned anything.

Hannah had spells of crying. "You are not worse off," Sarah Yetta tried to comfort her, "than so and so"—and she named women in their town whose daughters had committed suicide—"or those whose daughters have consumption. You ought to be much more hopeful than if I threw myself away on some worthless fellow."

"I trust in God and also in you that it will be right in the end, but now it has a bitter taste."

"A hard beginning, a good end," she said to cheer herself up as well as her mother.

Sarah Yetta went to her uncle Abram Loeb for the fifty roubles he had promised her. He lived in Hubovka, a village about fifteen miles from Elizavetgrad.

Abram Loeb's first wife had died of consumption. His second wife was always praying and lifting up her eyes to Heaven.

Though he was well-to-do, she would not let him educate her stepchildren; all they knew was what their grandfather Fivel had managed to teach them.

When Abram Loeb's eldest son was nineteen, she insisted that he marry a niece of hers. This niece was twenty-five and so ugly no one would have her. Abram Loeb forced his son to become engaged to her, but before the marriage his son became consumptive and died.

Abram Loeb's eldest daughter lost her husband six months after their marriage. When her son was born, she made up a lullaby that began,

"I forget he is dead and I think that he lives,

But when you cry, I remember our sorrow."

Dvoira, the youngest daughter, made up a song when she became engaged; the younger son also made up a song about his stepmother.

Dvoira had been engaged a long time. Her stepmother told Abram Loeb that Dvoira had all the clothes she needed, but all she had was a blouse and an old green skirt someone had pawned at her stepmother's for thirty-five copecks. The neighbors reproached Abram Loeb. At last he bought some cloth and had a tailor over from Elizavetgrad to make Dvoira a coat and a dress. His wife came from her room as the dress was tried on. A number of the neighbors had come in to gossip with the tailor. She went up to Dvoira and stooping, took the hem of the skirt in her hand.

"This is expensive cloth, isn't it?" she said sweetly.

"The best I could buy," said her husband.

She flushed and screamed before them all, "May you take it off her dead body!"

Abram Loeb stood up and struck the table so that the glasses jumped. "I have lived with you twenty years," he said, "and did not know until now that my children have a stepmother."

When Sarah Yetta came to Hubovka, Dvoira had become consumptive. Abram Loeb told Sarah Yetta that the doctors said that if Dvoira would go to Yalta, she might be cured. That would cost five hundred roubles and her husband did not have the money. Abram Loeb had, but his wife wanted him to spend it in having a scroll of the Torah written and placed in a synagogue in her name.

"But Uncle," Sarah Yetta said, "the life of a human being is more than another scroll of the Torah."

"You see," Abram Loeb answered, "your aunt has no children. All she would leave after her death is this scroll of the Torah. That is just as if she had a son."

"But isn't there time for that? Dvoira's sickness won't wait."

There were tears in her uncle's eyes and he looked wrinkled and old. "Don't tell anybody about this," he said. He promised to bring Sarah Yetta the fifty roubles, and she went off to see some acquaintances.

They told her of a strange thing that had happened: the son of a neighbor stole the eggs from the stork's nest on his father's barn and put goose eggs there instead for a joke; after the goslings were hatched, hundreds of storks flew over the barn, making a great racket; suddenly, they crowded down upon the nest and with their long bills tore the mother bird, goslings and nest to bits. When Sarah Yetta came to Hubovka, the barn had just burned to the ground, and no one knew how the fire had started.

Her uncle brought her the money, and in a few days she was off to America. The station was crowded: thirty families of Elizavetgrad were leaving for the New World. Hannah introduced her daughter to the Levitskys, and they promised her Sarah Yetta would be with them all the way to America.

In the train, Mrs. Levitsky told Sarah Yetta that their eldest son, Isaac, a friend of Sarah Yetta's brother Mordecai, had been in America a little over a year. Isaac had sent them all—there were six of them—steamship tickets. He was a tailor, and Sarah Yetta thought he must be doing well to be able to do that. Mrs. Levitsky's brother had given them money for their expenses to the steamer, but she was afraid they would not have enough. Sarah Yetta thought, Mordecai went to Odessa; why didn't he go to America with Isaac? My brothers are all cowards.

Sarah Yetta had only ninety-three roubles. She was told that she ought to have at least a hundred, but the Levitskys promised to help her, if they would receive money in Hamburg—Isaac had written that he would try to send them some. They put her baggage with theirs, and she did not have to bother with it.

She was so sick in the train they all thought she would turn back at Kremenchuk, because the worst was yet to come. It took them weeks to cross the border. It would have been no trouble for Sarah Yetta to get a passport to leave the country, but the Levitskys had two sons who would soon have had to serve in the army.

Most of their party were young men like that. From Kremenchuk they went down the Dnieper to Homel on a large raft. There they met the agent of the men in the business of helping emigrants across the border. He sent them to Wilna and from Wilna they went to Kovno. At Kovno they were bundled into a covered wagon and taken to a village. Here they rested a few days. They left in the wagon and travelled all night and most of the next day through fields and woods, uphill and downhill. In the middle of a field, a man stopped them and gave them each a passport. Sarah Yetta's was that of a man seventy years old, and a young man with them was given the passport of an old woman. It didn't matter, though. In broad daylight they rode into a German city, their baggage was examined, and they were free of Russia.

Here they had to pay their fares. Shestokovsky, who knew Sarah Yetta's brother Israel, asked her for twenty-five roubles until he could change a hundred-rouble bill. "I'll give you the twenty-five roubles tomorrow," he said.

"I cannot do it!" she answered. "I have just enough—and perhaps not enough—for the trip. I will not let any of it out of my hand."

"Well," he said, "hold the hundred-rouble bill until we can change it, and let me have twenty-five roubles."

"That I can do," she said.

When Sarah Yetta went for her steamship ticket in Hamburg, she found that she was five roubles short. And no money had come for the Levitskys. The boat for Glasgow was leaving the next day. They advised her to ask Shestokovsky to lend her five roubles—he had plenty—but she felt that she could not. "I'll sell my two pillows," she said. She had a good deal of trouble finding her baggage. As she began to unpack it, fifty roubles came for the Levitskys by telegraph. They lent her five, and she bought her ticket. She had just one copeck left, but she was on board the boat for Glasgow and would not need any money until she came to America.

The sea was so rough and so much water poured into the boat, the emigrants thought they would all be drowned. At Glasgow, they met the first people friendly to them on the journey. They gave the emigrants cider to refresh them after the boat trip, then a good supper and beds with clean sheets.

They were on the Atlantic for three weeks. Their ship was old and slow, and this was its last trip, they were told. Sometimes, there was a flood below deck. Sarah Yetta was very sick. She said all her psalms and prayers. Some of the people made fun of her, but she didn't care: when she said the psalms she felt better. As they came into the harbor of New York, the cabin passengers gathered on the upper deck and began to sing "Home, Sweet Home." Sarah Yetta understood the two words—like the Yiddish—and she and some of the others who knew it sang the Russian song beginning,

"I have forsaken my father's house;
The path to it is lost in the weeds."

At Castle Garden a doctor examined them. One of the Levitsky children was sickly, and they were all taken away. An official asked Sarah Yetta to whom she was going. A second cousin of her father's had given her the address of someone in New Haven. "Have you any money?" the official asked.

"Nothing."

He showed her where to get food and drink. He spoke a simple German she could understand. "After Yom Kippur"—that was the next day—"we will see what we can do with you." He spoke gently, and she thought him very kind.

Many of the women were waiting for their husbands. They promised to take Sarah Yetta with them. They stood, looking about, like birds in a cage. At four o'clock Sarah Yetta's name was called. She saw a gentleman outside. He doesn't know me, she thought. It must be somebody else with the same name.

The woman in charge came over to her. "*Mademoiselle,* this is your name, isn't it?"

"I thought it was somebody else with the same name," she said, and walked up to the stranger.

"I am Doctor Zolotarov," he said. "I don't know you, and you don't know me, but my father and your father were good friends. He wants me to bring you to his house."

"How does he know I am here?" she asked. She hesitated,

and then made up her mind not to go. "But how can I go with you if I don't know you?" she said.

"Do you know the Levitskys?" he asked. "I am taking them along with you."

The Zolotarovs were distant relatives of the Levitskys. When the Levitskys were held at Castle Garden, Isaac Levitsky went to Doctor Zolotarov to ask his help. Isaac happened to say that a girl had come with his parents, a Volsky, without relatives or friends in America. The doctor's father knew her father and asked the doctor to take her along.

The Zolotarovs lived on East Broadway. When Sarah Yetta and the Levitskys came there, the doctor's father was not at home. After their meal they went into the parlor; it was crowded with people to see the newcomers. Sarah Yetta didn't know anybody, though some had just come from Elizavetgrad. She envied the Levitskys because they had so many friends.

The doctor's father came in. Mr. Zolotarov had a long white beard and a good-natured, intelligent face. He shook hands with everybody and kissed the Levitskys. Then he sat down next to Sarah Yetta.

"Whose daughter are you, Abram Loeb's or Ezekiel's?"

"Ezekiel's."

"And how is your father?"

"My father has been dead for almost three years."

His eyes filled with tears. When he could speak, he told Sarah Yetta that her father had been one of his best friends. Mr. Zolotarov's father and mother had died when he was so young he could not remember them; at nine he was apprenticed to a tailor; and it was not until he was sixteen that he could begin to study the Bible and Talmud. Sarah Yetta's father used to help him in his studies. "Therefore," he said, "you are not to feel like a stranger in my house. Come to me for advice and help and whatever I can do for you, I will do. You are to think of me as your friend—as Ezekiel Volsky was mine." He asked her if she had any relative or friend in America. She could not remember any. She gave him the letter she had to the man in New Haven. Mr. Zolotarov knew him: he was a tailor. So was Mr. Zolotarov. Sarah Yetta told him that she had never worked at tailoring.

"The first thing to learn in America," he said, "is that you can do everything. You will learn how. The first thing to do is to *try*."

"What does *try* mean?"

"This is what it means: when you are asked if you can do a certain kind of work, say yes; sit down and do it as well as you can. If the boss or foreman doesn't like the way you do it, he sends you away, and you go to another place. By this time you know a little about it and you try again. If you like to work, you are sure to learn."

It became late, and Sarah Yetta wondered where they would put all the people. The doctor's mother came over to her and said, "Well, daughter, you are tired. Take a hot bath, here is a nightgown, and you'll sleep with me." It seemed to Sarah Yetta that she had come to the home of two angels, a beautiful old man and woman who cared for the troubled of all the world.

Sarah Yetta had a bath and was in Mrs. Zolotarov's soft warm bed when Mr. Zolotarov called to her. "I remember now that you have somebody here, a second cousin of yours, Simon Rubinov's son. I saw him last week."

"Yes, he's here! I know him well. He was my brother's partner."

"You'll find him at the Bershadskys'. Tomorrow is Yom Kippur and he'll be at home."

When Sarah Yetta woke, Mrs. Zolotarov had gone to synagogue. Sarah Yetta asked for Saul Rubinov's address. "You have had a good sleep," Mr. Zolotarov said. "It is almost eleven. Eat something before you go."

"I have fasted Yom Kippur since I was twelve," she said, "and I am twenty-three now. I have always thought it a sin to eat on Yom Kippur."

"But it's foolish to fast. You understand that, don't you?"

"I do not trouble myself about religious questions. I believe in what I was brought up to believe: I like it."

"Your father wasn't such a fool as you," said Mr. Zolotarov good-naturedly.

"But Father was religious."

"It's cold outside, and you're lightly dressed."

"I didn't bring any warm clothes. I was told that it was warm in America."

Mr. Zolotarov gave her his shawl. Mrs. Levitsky said to Isaac, "Take her there, so she won't lose her way."

When they were in the street, Isaac said, "Aren't you ashamed to walk with a tailor?" Sarah Yetta blushed. "Here you'll find that we are all tailors."

The Bershadskys lived on the fifth floor. Sarah Yetta asked for Saul Rubinov and told them that she was his cousin. Mr. Bershadsky said, "Saul went to synagogue. He's staying at my sister's now."

"Who is your sister?" she asked.

"Elka Budinov."

"She lived across the street from me! I made her children's clothes before she left." He gave Sarah Yetta her address. She wrote it on a slip of paper and asked Isaac for the address of the Zolotarovs. Sarah Yetta thanked him and told him that she did not want to make him come along. She asked her way of the passersby and came to the home of the Budinovs by herself.

When she opened the door, their four little daughters ran up to her, hugged her, and kissed her. The Budinovs shared a flat with another family. The men would buy men's old trousers, and in one of their rooms they cut and sewed them into trousers for boys. Mrs. Budinov and the other woman pressed the trousers and sewed the buttons on. They taught Saul how to use a sewing machine, and he was working with them. All this the eldest Budinov girl—she was about eleven—told Sarah Yetta happily. Now everybody was in synagogue.

Mr. Budinov came late in the afternoon. He went back to synagogue, and it wasn't long before Saul came. Mrs. Budinov said, "Stay with us. We are crowded anyway and what is one more? There are enough at the Zolotarovs'. You'll soon find work. I wish I knew as much as you." After they broke their fast, Saul and Sarah Yetta went to the Zolotarovs'. She thanked them for all they had done for her.

"Don't worry about how you are going to get on here," Mr. Zolotarov said to them. "America is a mother: she feeds you and clothes you and helps you in everything. I wrote a letter to New Haven," he said to Sarah Yetta, "but you mustn't sit around and wait for an answer. Look for work."

Next day she did. She was told where to go, but instead of turning to the right, she went to the left. Sarah Yetta walked on and on, looking at the crowds. She had never seen so many people. At Brooklyn Bridge, she watched them pouring out of the street-cars and the railway station. All strangers, she thought, and felt very lonely.

She walked on to William Street. At last she asked her way of an old man. He had just stepped out of a carriage. She spoke Yiddish and showed him the slip of paper on which she had her addresses. He walked with her all the way to Broadway and showed her how to go to Walker and Lispenard Streets. When she came there, it was late, and in all the shops she went to she was told, "No work."

She went back to the Zolotarovs'. They were as friendly as ever. Mr. Zolotarov worked quickly, a thousand stitches for a penny. Times were bad, he said, there was a financial panic in the country, but better times were coming. Sarah Yetta heard a man in the yard calling, "Line, line." What a sad voice, she thought, and went to the window: the man was in rags.

"What does he want?" she asked.

"What we all do," said Mr. Zolotarov. "Bread."

"Bread?"

"He is asking for clothes-lines to hang.... America is a blessed land, a land of great plenty, but it isn't regulated yet. The people have poured into this country from Europe, and some have too much and some not enough. Do you see this coat that I am making? I used to be paid eight dollars for it. Now I am paid only five. The Levitskys will make money, but I am an old man. I can make only one coat a week. That's five dollars. I must try to get better work, but it's hard to get any at all."

Some girls came in. Mrs. Zolotarov told them that Sarah Yetta had already been looking for work. They smiled and one said, "I have been looking for work for three months and can't find any." This frightened Sarah Yetta somewhat.

She went back to the Budinovs'. They were busy. Sarah Yetta threaded a needle and sewed on buttons. She helped set the table and wash the dishes and felt at home.

The next day was Saturday. Sarah Yetta did not want to look for work that day: she wanted to keep it as a day of rest. She went to the Zolotarovs'.

"It's lucky you came," Mr. Zolotarov said. "I have a letter from New Haven. They want you to go there. They have a son of fourteen or fifteen, and he is coming here to take you. Go home now and be ready."

The boy of fourteen or fifteen was tall and quite a young gentleman. Sarah Yetta was sorry for him—dragging her along in her European clothes, a grey coat and a white hat. She found his father and mother plain and simple and his sisters kind. They had been in America eight years and were doing well.

Sarah Yetta was to work for them for six dollars a week. They would keep two and half dollars of this for her board and lodging, and she was to have the rest in cash.

She had promised the Levitskys to begin to repay the five roubles they had lent her, and she owed Elka Budinov for board and lodging; but first she bought herself a pair of shoes—hers were worn out—and a hat for forty-nine cents. And the next week she sent her mother three dollars.

Sarah Yetta began to feel that her work did not please the people she was with. She had never worked for a tailor, and at this time they had only coats and furs to fix. In a few weeks, too, the work slackened. She thought it would be better for her to work in a factory. She could do best at waists, shirts, or wrappers. But in New Haven there were only corset factories.

On a Monday, after she had been in New Haven five weeks, they had little to do in the shop. The younger daughter said to Sarah Yetta, "Let's go home and work at home." They told her that there was a lot of washing to do. Sarah Yetta did not mind washing the clothes of her own family, but she did not like to do it for others. She had helped with the dishes and about the house, but this was hard for her to stomach. But she thought that she ought not to feel that way about it—she was one of the family—and she washed their clothes.

In another week they had no work in the shop, not even for themselves. They advised Sarah Yetta to stay with them until after Christmas; then they would try to find work for her in a corset factory. Beginners were paid five dollars a week. Sarah Yetta thought that she could do much better at work she knew. Besides, she liked New York better than New Haven. New Haven reminded her of Elizavetgrad. She was told that she would have to do what everybody else did—buy a new coat on payments to be dressed like the others.

She told the tailor's father that she would be sorry to leave New Haven for one thing—she did not have to work Saturdays. She did not know what she would have to do in New York. "But my children are going to work Saturdays," he said. "They want to build up the business."

In New York Sarah Yetta found that the small shops in which she looked for a job were working long hours, from seven in the morning until ten at night; and at that she could not find work. Business in the factories was at its dullest before Christmas.

She lived at the Budinovs'. She had saved some money in New Haven, and she paid the Levitskys what she owed. She had her pillows there, and they wanted her to take them away, but she had no place to put them. One day at the Levitskys', she met an old man who knew all her people. "You have a rich relative here named Shlikerman," he said.

"Yes," Sarah Yetta said, "now I remember that my father once wrote a letter to a Mrs. Shlikerman."

"I'll give you her address, and you go there."

"I want to find a job first."

She found work sewing flannels. Even experienced help did not do well at that work. After a bad day she came home to find them all excited. Mrs. Shlikerman had been to see her. She left word that she was not to go to work next day, and a friend of hers would bring Sarah Yetta to her house. "I can't go there now," Sarah Yetta said. "I'll lose my job."

She received a letter from home. They wrote that they were doing well. She knew that it was not true, but she could not help them.

One day she was told that there was no more work and

came home in the morning. She went to Mrs. Shlikerman's friend and was taken to Brooklyn. Mrs. Shlikerman looked like her sister whom Sarah Yetta had known in Russia. She was very friendly and said that Sarah Yetta must stay with her for a rest. She told Sarah Yetta that she could not find work until after Christmas, and that then she would find work for her. "I have many acquaintances," Mrs. Shlikerman said. "In the meantime you will not have to be idle." She gave Sarah Yetta slip-covers to make. Sarah Yetta also had a chance to fix her coat: it was not very warm, but it did not look so bad.

The slip-covers took her about a week to cut and sew. She found Mr. Shlikerman—a clever, learned, and good man—as interesting as Mr. Zolotarov. Saul Rubinov came to see them, and he and Mr. Shlikerman became friends.

Mrs. Shlikerman found work for her in Brooklyn; one of Mrs. Shlikerman's friends took Sarah Yetta to Siegel-Cooper's factory. Its sewing machines were run by electricity, and the forewoman had to show her how to use the machine. Sarah Yetta understood a little English, but could not speak any. The forewoman spoke at the top of her voice. Sarah Yetta smiled and by gestures made her understand that she was dumb but not deaf; the forewoman laughed and became friendlier.

In about ten minutes Sarah Yetta could run the machine and was given part of a nightgown to sew. The operators did not make all of the gown—some sewed one part, some another: this was called "section work." There were five dozen of the part Sarah Yetta had to sew in her bundle and when she was through, the forewoman marked it in a little book.

A tall woman sat at the machine next to Sarah Yetta's. When the forewoman was gone, her neighbor asked to see Sarah Yetta's book. She showed Sarah Yetta by signs that she should have been given twenty cents more for each dozen and that she should speak to the forewoman about it. Sarah Yetta did not know what to do. If she complained, she might get her neighbor into trouble. In the morning Sarah Yetta brought her a note. In this Sarah Yetta had written for her that she did not wish to say anything about the price she was paid, because she did not want to lose the job.

The girl to her left, across the aisle, made fun of Sarah Yetta. There was only one other Jewish girl in the place, and she would not talk to Sarah Yetta—afraid the girls would make fun of her too. But the woman next to Sarah Yetta brought her a cup and gave her some tea at lunch. She tried to teach Sarah Yetta the names of what they made and used: sleeves, collars, bands, needle, thread, and the like. Sarah Yetta wanted to find out how long her neighbor was in America. She learned the words of the question and asked it. Her neighbor answered that her grandparents were born in America. Then Sarah Yetta asked her what the other girls were. She said that they were foreigners—Irish, Italians, and Bohemians. One day she took Sarah Yetta's book to the forewoman and demanded that Sarah Yetta be paid in full. Her neighbor came back and told her to look for work elsewhere: now there was work everywhere. And Sarah Yetta did not see her again.

Saturday afternoon Sarah Yetta went to Mrs. Shlikerman— she had given Sarah Yetta a place to board at as soon as she had begun to work at Siegel-Cooper's—and told Mrs. Shlikerman what the woman at the machine next to her had said. Mrs. Shlikerman took Sarah Yetta to a Mr. Kass, who had a large store in New York and knew many manufacturers.

Monday morning Mr. Kass went with Sarah Yetta to a factory on Walker Street. They had no machine for her, but would have one in about a week. Nathan Bershadsky advised her to work where he was a cutter. There they made shirts of the best silks and flannels. But Sarah Yetta did not want to be a worker always. It seemed to her that at waists or wrappers she would have a chance to be in business for herself. However, she worked with Nathan Bershadsky a few days, until she received a postcard from the place on Walker Street.

The foreman there was a tall, pale, nervous man. He gave Sarah Yetta a waist to sew, and when she brought it to his table, looked it over and without a word gave her a bundle of waists to make. The other girls were much faster than she. She was not used to sewing without basting. It seemed to her that European ways were a century behind those in America.

One day, a new waist came into style. It was gathered in front and at the collar. The foreman had the goods gathered and then cut it; but when the waists were made, the gathering was out of place. He blamed the girls. The designer was sent for and showed some of the girls how to place the gathering. Only the best hands could do it, and it was such a bother that they would not.

Sarah Yetta finished her bundle of work, and the foreman gave her the new waist to sew. She told him that she used to make waists like that in Russia without any trouble, but he would have to cut them differently. She cut one waist, and it was good. He asked her what she knew of cutting. She told him that she had studied Glazhdinsky's system and had brought the books with her. "You will have to find another place," he said to her the next day. "I cannot have you around: everybody saw you showing me how to make that waist." He gave her an address on Lispenard Street; a Mr. Wolfman was in need of a designer, and she would do well there. Sarah Yetta was sorry that she had not held her tongue.

Mr. Wolfman set her to work at wrappers. She was paid six dollars a week.

* * *

Sarah Yetta was living again with the Budinovs'. In about nine months they moved to another street. Their rooms were on the top floor. She found it hard to climb the stairs, and the smell in the hall was sickening. Saul Rubinov was still working for them. His bed was in the same room as the sewing-machines.

That summer was hot, hotter than usual, people said. One day at half past five Mr. Wolfman sent his help home. In other shops girls had fainted from the heat. That day Sarah Yetta counted the steps she had to climb: there were seventy-two. When she came in, to her surprise Saul and Mr. Budinov stopped work. They washed themselves and praised the water. "This is a blessed land," said Mr. Budinov at the sink, "the water flows from the walls, all the water you want."

After supper, when no one else was about, Saul asked Sarah Yetta to walk with him to Brooklyn Bridge. "I cannot work any more today," he said. "That is the only place to get a little fresh air." As they walked to the bridge, he said, "Do you think I ought to become engaged?" She knew that a relative of his was anxious to have Saul marry his daughter. Sarah Yetta thought it a good thing for Saul. The girl was good-looking, and her family well off. She had a dowry of five hundred dollars and was fond of him. A week before she had come with tickets to a theater party. Saul said that he would take two. "Why two?" she asked. "I have one." "I'll take my cousin, too," he said, and turned to Sarah Yetta. The girl had not liked that, but Sarah Yetta thought it nice of him. The girl's father was with her and asked Sarah Yetta jokingly, "How does a girl happen to come to America all by herself?" She had been afraid of that question. Her mother had said that she would meet it everywhere. "If I had been asked that at Castle Garden, where no one knew me," she answered earnestly, "I might have jumped into the water; but in this house I am well known. Mrs. Budinov left

Elizavetgrad only three weeks before I did." Sarah Yetta thought Saul had this man's daughter in mind, and she said, "It's a good idea. They'll put you on your feet, and you won't have to work so hard."

He gave her an angry look. "I'll get on my feet myself. I want nobody's help. My father and mother wanted to send me money, but I would not take it. But can I become engaged when I am making only seven dollars and fifty cents a week?"

"If you like each other, it won't matter. She won't want anything of you."

In the meantime they reached the bridge. They found a bench and rested. The air was cool and refreshing. Saul went on to say that he would not marry until he had saved some money and could go into business for himself. Sarah Yetta said that he was right and that he would do well, for he had a good head on his shoulders. "Well, then," he said, "good luck to us!" and took her hand.

"What are you talking about?" she managed to say.

"Have you anything against me?"

"Nothing, but this is no match for you. You know how poor I am, and I must help my family too; and I am not doing as well in America as I thought I should. I am not strong, and I do not want you to be burdened with me."

At last they agreed to say nothing to anyone until Saul had the consent of his father and mother. "In the meantime," Sarah Yetta said, "you will have enough time to make up your mind. Nobody need know, and if you change your mind, nobody will be hurt." They came home late. The night was so hot no one could sleep, and in the morning each went to work.

That night Mrs. Budinov did not answer Sarah Yetta when she said, "Good-evening." She thought Mrs. Budinov was troubled about something and had not heard her. But when Sarah

Yetta spoke to her afterwards and she did not answer, Sarah Yetta said, "Elka, are you angry at me?"

"Yes," she answered. "I never thought you were so false.

"In what way?"

"You are engaged to Saul, and you never told me a word."

Saul heard them, and came out of the room where he worked. "I told Elka," he said.

She did not believe that they had become engaged only the night before—if they did become engaged. "You are hiding things from me," she said. "I thought you were my friend."

From then on Sarah Yetta found her quarrelsome. In the autumn the Budinovs were to move from four rooms to three. This means, Sarah Yetta thought, that they do not want me. Next door were the Rothsteins, and she arranged to sleep with their daughter. It was not comfortable.

Then Saul quarrelled with the Budinovs. He and Shestokovsky became partners and they went to New Haven. Sarah Yetta was still working at Wolfman's for six dollars a week. She was good at samples, but other girls made two dozen wrappers in the time she could only make three quarters of a dozen. One day she said to the girl next to her, "I'm only making six dollars a week."

"What!" she screamed, "I'm doing three times as much as you, and I make five and a half!" And what a hullabaloo she raised! Mr. Wolfman called Sarah Yetta into his office and scolded her. She was to have no more than five dollars a week from then on, he said. But she could not get along on that.

Mr. Rothstein suggested that she work for a contractor he knew, a Mr. Hyamson. Hyamson had a place in a cellar. He said that if Sarah Yetta made the trimmings and set in the yokes, she could work there, and took her into a side room to his wife. She had given birth to a child the week before. She had been making the pleating, but now she could only baste it and her husband finished it. Sarah Yetta showed them how to make pleatings without basting and ironing. The Hyamons were intelligent. But how poor they were! And they looked consumptive.

When their workers came—there were six of them—each looked as if she would smash everything about her. The girl opposite Sarah Yetta had the boldest face of all. She told Sarah Yetta that she was a socialist and a "union lady." Mr. Hyamson was afraid of her, gave her work first, and what she said went. She told Sarah Yetta what she would like to do to "bosses."

"This one, too?" Sarah Yetta asked.

"A boss is a boss. He'll work himself up and be like the rest."

Hyamson went away to the warehouse. At four o'clock several bundles of work were delivered. Next morning Sarah Yetta came early. On every machine Hyamson had prepared work for the day. The girl opposite Sarah Yetta made the collars. These happened to be of silk with a stiffening of buckram. She put the buckram on top; as she sewed, the silk came together underneath and each collar had buckram—almost two inches of it— over. This she cut off. Sarah Yetta thought it best not to say anything, but at last she could not keep still. "Excuse me, Miss," she said, "you are spoiling the collars. They won't fit."

"Do you know what mind your own business means?" she answered.

"Yes."

"Well, then, do it."

There were ten dozen wrappers in all. The next operator sewed the collars on and gathered in the two inches. And the work went out this way. Hyamson was called to the warehouse. When he came back, he told them that he would not be given

more work until this was made right. But the girls would not
help him.

"What are you all angry about?" Sarah Yetta said to them.
"Put a wrapper on." A girl did, and, of course, she could not
button the collar. "Would you buy a wrapper like this?" Sarah
Yetta asked.

Hyamson went to the machine of the girl who made the collars, opened the drawer, and took out the pieces of buckram she
had cut off. "Here is my trouble," he said. He begged the girls
to stay and help him with the wrappers, but they would not.

Sarah Yetta helped him, but she said, "I won't be able to be
here any longer: the girls will kill me." I should work for the
manufacturer instead of a contractor, she thought. She asked
Hyamson for the manufacturer's address, went there, and was
given work to do at home.

The Rothsteins had moved into the Budinovs' old flat. The
extra room was Saul's. He had come from New Haven, sick, and
without money. A relative of his lent him twenty-five dollars.
He bought a stock of old trousers and made them into trousers
for boys. Sarah Yetta had a sewing-machine in her room, and
there she made her wrappers, but was poorly paid. A girl who
lived on the floor below also worked at wrappers, and she told
Sarah Yetta of Levy and Lillienthal on Lispenard Street. "It
would be better for you to work for them," she said. "They pay
well. You are careful, and they want that kind."

But one morning Mr. Wolfman sent for her and offered her
the old job at seven dollars a week. Saul advised her to take it:
she would not have to carry bundles home and to the factory.
By this time Sarah Yetta could make any wrapper.

She had a letter from home. They were not doing well. And
Saul was not doing well. He could not sell his stock of boys'
trousers and had no money to buy old trousers.

One Saturday, as she was working in Wolfman's, Sarah Yetta watched the men cutting up thick layers of cloth and the expressmen hauling the bundles away. These are going to contractors like Hyamson, she thought, and people who do not know how to sew a seam, and here am I working for seven dollars a week. She made up her mind to go to Levy and Lillienthal that day and to try to get work for Sunday. Mr. Wolfman wanted her to work overtime or to take work home, but she told him she had something to do.

Levy and Lillienthal had a nice, sunny place on the first floor. A red-bearded man came up to Sarah Yetta. "I want to see the boss," she said.

"I am the boss."

"I want work."

"I have no work for you. That's all!" and he walked away.

A boy was sweeping the floor. She asked him who that was.

"Levy," he said.

"I want to see Mr. Lillienthal."

Mr. Lillienthal cocked his head and looked at her; he was cross-eyed. "I made up my mind not to give any more work to Jews," he said.

"How do you know my work is as bad as that of others? I know it is said one Jew is answerable for another; but if that is so, you are answerable for your partner who almost chased me out of the place, because I asked for work. Try me," Sarah Yetta said.

"For whom do you work?"

"I am making samples for Mr. Wolfman. I am paid seven dollars a week, but that is not enough for me. I must help my family in Russia. I did this work in Russia and had eight girls working for me."

Mr. Lillienthal said in a gentler voice, "I'll show you why we refused you work," and led her into the showroom. "This is the kind of work they do," and he brought her up to a wrapper on a figure.

Sarah Yetta told him what was wrong: the wrapper was of a soft goods and the contractor had used a long stitch that pulled the wrapper out of shape. "You must know how to do this work," she said.

"I'll give you half a dozen of these wrappers. Bring them tomorrow. What time will you be here?

"Early in the afternoon."

"I pay two dollars and sixty-five cents a dozen for this style." Her eyes sparkled.

Next day she was up at dawn. She finished the work early. She could hardly wait for the afternoon. Saul and Rothstein made fun of her. They told her not to be so happy. "You think you're going to be a capitalist," said Rothstein, "but you don't know the bosses."

"And you don't know the workers," Sarah Yetta said.

Only Levy, Lillienthal, a woman, and a packer were in the place. Sarah Yetta opened her bundle. Mr. Lillienthal called the woman over. "Very good work," she said in English. "Very fine, very fine."

Lillienthal turned to Sarah Yetta. "I am going to send you five dozen of these to make. Have you any other work?"

"No."

"How soon will you deliver it?"

"As quickly as I can. I can bring you some before all are finished, if you want me to."

"Are you doing this work yourself?"

"Yes, but I'll have someone to help me later."

"I warn you," he said, "against hiring men."

Tears in her eyes, Sarah Yetta thanked him for the work. He shook hands with her and said, "I am sure you will be a success in this country."

She went home and rested. At half-past four her work came. She could not keep from opening a bundle. She made the collars and belts that day and brought the wrappers back Wednesday morning. They were examined, and she was paid fourteen dollars and fifty-eight cents.

When she came home, Saul was lying on the couch. He had walked about all morning trying to sell the boys' trousers he had made. "How is your work?" she asked.

He shook his head. "I see you're happy," he said.

Sarah Yetta gave him the money. "Deposit it. And I'm to receive another bundle of work soon."

"What have you there?

"Half a dozen samples. He pays me fifty cents a sample. He's an angel!"

She sat down at her machine. Saul walked about the room. Sarah Yetta was afraid that if she asked him to join her at the work, he would be sure not to. She knew how touchy he was, and that he thought her too ready to tell everybody what to do.

In a few days he happened to say that he hated to use her money for buying the old trousers he made into trousers for boys. "It isn't mine," she said. "There is no mine and yours; it's ours. But please listen to me: here you are at a dirty work— buying old trousers and making them into trousers for children —why, that's criminal! Why should you do that when at my work we have such a future? It's not tailoring; it's not work you ought to be ashamed of. I have my cutting books. You can learn the wrapper trade right here, and when you know that, there are plenty of places where they want young men like you. And you are so good at figures! I see you've made up your mind not to do it, because you think it's against your dignity. You ought to see what foolish contractors there are: I heard one of them trying to excuse himself to Lillienthal—the buttons had fallen off his wrappers. I am slow at sewing the long seams.

With your energy, if you would only run off the seams for me, we could make three times as much. In a few weeks I am sure you will make a wrapper as well as I. Then you can do what you like—work here or get a job. In time you might be a manufacturer: you've been in business."

Saul was wild with anger. He called her whatever he could think of, walked up and down the room, and talked and talked. "Well, don't do it," she said, "if you don't want to; this is a free country." But when the next bundle of work was brought, he opened it and took everything out carefully. While she was finishing the work she still had to do, he made the collars and belts.

In a few weeks she asked Mr. Lillienthal, "How do you like my work?"

"It's very good," he said.

"Well, a man is doing most of it. He's a second cousin of mine. He's an educated man; he was not a workingman in Russia, but here he worked at knee-pants. I want you to make his acquaintance, and all our transactions can be through him. I will have more time, then, for your better work and your samples."

When Saul went to see Mr. Lillienthal, it was raining. The street-car would not stop for him, and he came there dripping wet. As he bent down to undo the bundle, the water ran off his derby upon the wrappers. Lillienthal noticed this and scolded him. Saul came home angry: he would never go there again.

Sarah Yetta went the next time, and reminded Mr. Lillienthal that Saul had not been a workingman in Russia, and was not used to being talked to in that way; soaking wet, he could not help a little clumsiness; and, after all, Mr. Lillienthal ought to forgive such little things in greenhorns. Saul went again to Lillienthal, and this time they had a long talk: Mr. Lillienthal said he would give them a quarter more on a dozen, if they would do their work as well as they had been doing. She seldom went to Lillienthal's after that.

One Saturday, when they paid Mrs. Rothstein their rent, she told them that from then on it would be eleven dollars. Saul said, "But you pay only twelve for all the rooms."

"You are making money," she answered, "and I want that much."

Sarah Yetta and Saul used to take Saturday afternoon off to rest up, and he said, "Let's go for a walk." It was late in the fall, and the weather was blustery. "I'm going to look for rooms," he said.

"But how can we?"

"You'll stay there until I fix up a place. Must we work in that tiny bedroom without air and the watercloset five floors down?"

They found three rooms—a sink and washtubs in the kitchen, and the water-closet in the hall—at ten dollars a month. And the house was much cleaner than where they lived. As they walked down the stairs, an old woman stopped them and asked, "Would you let one room to a woman with two children whose husband makes little? They can't pay much."

Saul said that he could let the kitchen. That was just what the woman wanted: it was a big, sunny room.

"What do you want for this room?" she asked.

"What can you pay?" Saul answered.

"What can I pay? I can pay three dollars. But what do you want?"

She could not believe that they were satisfied with three dollars, and promised Saul to keep the kitchen door closed so that the children would not bother him while he was working. The old woman then introduced Sarah Yetta and Saul to her daughter. She lived on the floor below. They hired the old woman to cook for them—she wanted to do it for nothing— and her daughter to sew buttons on the wrappers.

That evening Saul moved their machines and packages to Allen Street. Then they bought two beds. One was put into the bedroom—that was Sarah Yetta's—and the other, a folding bed, was Saul's. This went into the room where they were to work. Saul had insisted that Sarah Yetta move there too. "We don't have to pay people to watch over us," he said. "We can watch over ourselves." In their new quarters they could work as long as they liked; they worked, sometimes, from three in the morning until twelve at night.

A little before Passover, Sarah Yetta received a letter from her mother. In it was the address of a cousin who lived in Brownsville, Brooklyn. Saul said that on Passover they would not work for two days: they would make a holiday of it and visit their cousin.

Brownsville had open fields on all sides, except one, and the air was sweet and clean. The elevated trains that ran on Allen Street used soft coal, and the smoke blew into their windows and choked Sarah Yetta. They could rent a store and three rooms in Brownsville, their cousin told them, for only eight dollars a month.

But Mr. Lillienthal did not want them to move to Brownsville: it would take another day to bring the goods there and back. Saul showed him how they could hire help—other contractors had shops in Brownsville—and their deliveries would be better. Saul had come to think that he did not want to be a "boss" and have others work for him; but he was anxious to please Lillienthal.

So they moved to Brownsville. That summer Sarah Yetta had a letter from home that made her cry. She saw no way out of their troubles but for her mother, sister, and youngest brother to come to America. "Let us marry first," said Saul, "and then we'll see what both of us can do for your family."

They were married in September. Sarah Yetta went to all their friends and asked them to the wedding. She asked Elka Budinov to be matron-of-honor and her husband to be Saul's best man. They were still unfriendly, but Sarah Yetta begged their forgiveness and thanked them for all they had done, and at last they said they would come. The Levinskys, the Bershadskys, the Shlikermans and the Zolotarovs were at the wedding too: Sarah Yetta was sure that there had never been as many intelligent people in Brownsville before. Next door lived the Levinsons, excellent people! They had come from Moscow, and were in the United States about a year and a half. Mrs. Levinson and Sarah Yetta's cousin prepared the food. A rabbi married Saul and Sarah Yetta. Some of their friends, who were radicals, made fun of them for having a wedding, but Sarah Yetta said, "I am not going to be among the first to jump away from the old customs: who knows where I'd land?"

They wrote Sarah Yetta's mother of their plan for bringing her and the younger children to the United States; but Hannah's answer was unlike her other letter: Mordecai had come from Odessa, Abram and Rachmiel were helping her somewhat, Israel would soon be through with his service in the army, and Frieda had a wonderful offer. A young man wanted to marry her without any dowry at all. "A girl like Frieda," Hannah wrote, "does not have to go to America: she can marry where she is. And please, my daughter, do not ask the other children to come to you. I do not want to go to America; do not tear my children away from me."

One day Saul came from New York and said, "Levy and Lillienthal have no more work for anybody: they are giving up their partnership. I went somewhere else. The new work looks hard to me; I do not think we'll do as well." And they did not. They thought it would help them to sell retail too. So they moved to another street: the rent was a dollar less and the neighborhood better for a retail store. But in a few weeks they received a postcard from Lillienthal: he had gone into business for himself. Though times were bad, he gave them plenty of work.

Sarah Yetta made up her mind to have nothing to do with their new neighbors. The husband, a young man, wore a beard; his wife had her hair bobbed. One Saturday night, in the spring, Sarah Yetta was not well, but she did not want Saul to stay at home because of her. He went to the Bershadskys', and she was studying English. Someone knocked at the door. It was their neighbor. "I see that you have plenty of work," she said, "can you let me have something to do? My husband is on strike, and all we made last week was thirty-five cents. We haven't a thing to live on."

"If your husband can operate a sewing machine—there is no strike in our line—he can work here."

"Thank you," her neighbor said, "but I do not think my husband would care for your kind of work."

Sarah Yetta asked her to sit down, but she would not. Her manner seemed to say, I will have as little as possible to do with you; I only want work. When Saul came home, Sarah Yetta told him of the visit. He blamed her: she should have been friendly to their neighbors; they might die of hunger and she, with plenty of everything, did not care what they were doing; she should have been to visit them first.

Sarah Yetta was up early in the morning and opened the kitchen door a number of times to hear if her neighbors were up. Perhaps they are dying of hunger, she thought. At last she heard voices: they were not dead yet. She knocked at the door and was asked in. She apologized for not having come before, and made some excuse or other; then she told their neighbor that he could work with them until the strike was over. His wife could not do much: she was about to have another child; but she could sew buttons on the wrappers.

The minute their neighbor moved his machine into their

place, he became very friendly. Whenever Saul and Sarah Yetta had something to say to each other, he had something to say too. He claimed to be a socialist. As soon as he earned a dollar (Saul did not pay him wages, but gave him all that Lillienthal paid for the work) he would work no more that day, even if it was only two o'clock. "Six dollars a week is enough for me and my family," he would say. "I am not going to make the bosses rich. You are fools to do more." He would put his feet on the machine and read his Yiddish newspaper.

"In New York," he would say, "you can get along without English. Why trouble your head to learn it?"

His wife gave birth to another girl. While she was in labor, he went off to a socialist meeting and did not come back until midnight. Sarah Yetta moved near the Levinsons again, but she was not rid of their neighbor. He moved his sewing machine along with their machines.

In August, Sarah Yetta gave birth to her eldest child. She had a hard time. Before his birth, Mrs. Levinson was by her side for three days; the night after, the Levinsons had no hot supper: Mrs. Levinson had not slept the night before and had had so much trouble with Sarah Yetta she could not do another thing. Sarah Yetta wondered how one could be so good to a stranger, and how glad she was to have a son to name after her father.

Brownsville was growing; traveling to and from New York was hard, but many chose to live in the sunshine and fresh air of Brownsville, rather than among the tenements of the East Side. Times were good; there was work for everybody.

One evening her old neighbor with the bobbed hair came to see Sarah Yetta. She said that Sarah Yetta ought not to help

Saul at the wrappers. Sarah Yetta explained that what she did was easy for her but hard for him, and that she liked to do it. Sarah Yetta was too devoted to Saul, the other said, and was a bad example. I must be rid of these people, Sarah Yetta thought; so she said, "Your husband is not here now, and I can talk freely. He does me harm and himself harm. There was a time when he could not work at his trade; that time is over. He's a tailor; let him go back to his tailoring. It will be much better for you. You don't have to work. He isn't doing enough."

Her husband came to work next morning at ten o'clock. Sarah Yetta walked in from the kitchen and said to Saul, "We did a favor to this gentleman, but now we'll ruin him. A married man of thirty-five who has two children and comes to work at ten o'clock has lost his bearings. Let him go to his tailoring; among his own people he'll be ashamed to act like this." Saul was surprised at her. But she insisted that the fellow take his machine away. That night he and his wife came to tell Saul and Sarah Yetta that he had found a job at twelve dollars a week. They were moving to New York. Good riddance! Sarah Yetta thought.

A few months after Ezekiel was born, Saul was called to Lillienthals'. Mr. Lillienthal asked him to be his foreman. Saul was uncertain. Ought he to join the forces of Capital? Sarah Yetta thought that he should take the position; by refusing it, he would not change the capitalistic system. He would be helpful and fair; in this position he could be of more help to the workers than in any other. Some of his friends thought otherwise: to be a workingman was nobler. But Sarah Yetta told Saul that he had worked with hands and feet from six in the morning until late at night for years; that was enough. How long would a man last working like that? He was the father of a son and it was his duty to better himself if he could.

So Saul became Henry Lillienthal's foreman. In two weeks

he was disheartened. The work was a strain, he had to be on his feet all day, and he was between two millstones, on one side the workers, on the other the "boss": each had to be satisfied. "This is your problem," Sarah Yetta said, "and you must solve it. It is a great opportunity and more future to it than sitting in your own house." But travelling from and to Brownsville was hard; Saul wanted her to move to New York, and they did.

One day Sarah Yetta had bad news from home. A little while before she and Saul had sent her elder brother money to come to America—Michael had never been able to get along—and now they had a letter that he could not come: he had consumption.

They had Ezekiel and themselves photographed. Saul addressed the envelopes and left the photographs for Sarah Yetta to mail. She saw that there was none for her elder brother. Saul had once quarrelled with Michael's wife, and Sarah Yetta thought that he was not sending Michael a photograph because of that. How silly, she thought, how cruel! and Michael is sick. When Saul came home that evening, she told him all that. "Michael is dead," he said. One of her brothers had written them, but Saul had kept the letter from Sarah Yetta.

They lived across the street from a public school. One day one of their cousins who had just come from Russia was in their house. At three o'clock, when school was over for the day, all the children came running out—so many of them—and his eyes filled with tears. Sarah Yetta remembered how she, too, had longed for an education. "We are a lost generation," she said. "It is for our children to do what they can."

PART TWO

Ezekiel had made the Forty-second Street library his hang-out. He had walked the streets through shine and rain and a Jonah in the belly of the wind; at home had dodged his father's glances. Now he flung away his wishes as a bother: he would do whatever he wanted. To begin with, he would be in business for himself. He was through working for others—when he worked.

He knew of a basement store in Greenwich Village. The street was only a block long and ran in a half-circle from one quiet street to another. So much the better, he thought, for the bookstore he had in mind. The store had been empty a long time, ever since he could remember.

He was aware of his creased and baggy clothes, shiny with the hours he had improved in the chairs of the library. He felt the wide-open mouth in the sole of each shoe and reasoned with himself that only the pavement knew his secret. What have you to lose? he kept urging himself.

Too late. He had rung the bell. The door opened, and a woman looked at him as if he were about to steal the doormat. He almost laughed in her face. "Whom can I see about renting the store in the basement?"

"The grocer around this corner, the first store you come to."

The grocery was small. The grocer was a little man in an apron too large for him, dirty at the waist. Ezekiel felt strong in his own height. A little girl on rollerskates, waiting for her order, kept making a racket on the wooden floor and banging into the barrels. Ezekiel waited.

Two women came in. He could not walk out like that, could he? The grocer might think he had stolen something. "Well?" the grocer turned on him.

"I want to rent the store you have for rent around the corner." Ezekiel heard his voice falter, and he should not have repeated *rent* like that, but the grocer wasn't a stylist.

"Thirty-five a month. Two months' security." The voice was matter-of-fact.

"I'll wait until you finish waiting on your customers."

The grocer turned to the two women, and Ezekiel put the brakes on his whirling mind to rest before the next lap.

When the grocer was through, Ezekiel said, "I can't give you any security, because I haven't any money. I want to rent the store for a bookstore. I believe I can get books on credit. If I can't—if I do business, you'll get your rent. You can't get anybody to rent your store, anyway; it's been empty a long time. You have nothing to lose by letting me in and everything to gain."

"And suppose somebody with money comes along to rent it?"

"What's to stop you? I'm not asking you for a lease now. You can put me out any time."

The grocer hesitated. Then a customer came in, and the grocer turned with relief to the familiar taking down of a bottle and cans, wrapping them, and dropping the money into the cash-register, where it clinked a pleasant echo to the loud bell.

No other customers came in, and Ezekiel was standing there. "Well, I'll try you," the grocer said. The cash register sang out again. He took a key from the back of the drawer and slid it reluctantly across the counter.

Ezekiel felt for the key in his pocket every other instant. There was a little hole in that pocket. Suppose the key fell through? There were holes in the other pockets also. He decided to hold the key in his fist and his fist in his pocket. How smooth the key was, except for the sharp corners where it fitted into the lock.

He heard a noise far behind, but walked on. The shouting grew. A woman was looking at him out of a window, and a group of children had stopped playing to watch him. He looked behind. There was the grocer, motioning him back.

The grocer was still somewhat out of breath. "I haven't even got your name."

Ezekiel gave him his name and spelled it; then his address. The grocer tore off a piece of wrapping paper—not along the bar, but a jagged piece—wet the point of his pencil in his mouth and wrote in a clumsy hand.

"You're a Jew?"

Ezekiel was tempted to say no. If he said yes, the grocer might not let him have the store. Anyway, he would not be friendly. The question was not friendly. But if he said no, and the grocer would still suspect him a Jew, even if he never found out that he was, he might never be able to win his friendship. But if he knew him to be a Jew, could he ever win that? To hell with his friendship! He must show him that he was not afraid of him. "Yes," Ezekiel answered calmly, regretting the hesitation.

The grocer said nothing, but folded up the piece of paper and put it in the drawer where the key had been.

He too would say nothing, Ezekiel thought, until his castle was built and all the banners flying. Then he would invite the family to behold. He could see his father lifting up his face in surprise. This I, your worthless son, have built; this is mine, and all these lawns and streams and woods, this park is mine— and yours!

* * *

Ezekiel reached the stoop of the tenement in which he lived and entered the dark, familiar smell. The janitor's wife—to ward off her trouble she had clothed herself in layers and balloons of fat —was floundering on the stairs like a mammal out of the deep sea. She threw an angry glance after Ezekiel as his feet left stains on the newly washed wood. "Can I help it?" he apologized.

"A nice time to come home—in the middle of the day." And she went on scrubbing, muttering curses she would not have uttered a syllable of, if there were any likelihood of their coming true.

Ezekiel was glad to find that his mother was not at home. His two brothers, too young to go to school, were playing on the floor with pots and pans dragged out of the kitchen closet. The younger, just then, was sitting disconsolately in a pool. Ezekiel searched for the scrubbing brush and wrapped it in a newspaper together with a box of scouring powder and a bar of yellow soap (that had been washed from its pristine square into a smooth, matronly waistline). With these under his arm he passed the janitor's wife, who had now reached the tiles of the two-by-four vestibule.

Then he saw that he had forgotten rags to use as a mop, and a pail would be handy. He went back, put everything in the pail and wrapped that in the newspaper, a bundle no longer as genteel as at first.

He hurried towards the store. Now and then he felt for the key in his pocket. Why hadn't he eaten when he was at home? He was weak and shaky. Well, he wouldn't go back. He walked another block and a half. It was no use. He must eat, otherwise he wouldn't have strength to do the cleaning. And he had forgotten the broom. Couldn't he have sat down calmly and thought

out all that he needed instead of snatching up a few things,
and then hurrying back and snatching up a few things more?

His mother would be home by this time. She would come in
and see the mess on the floor, put down her bags and bundles,
catch up the youngsters and give them a few slaps. Then she
would look for a rag to wipe the floor, and find the rags gone
and the pail gone—he smiled at her bewilderment.

But when he got home, his mother had not yet come. He
lit the gas and put the kettle on, and cut himself a thick slice
of black bread. His brothers at once set up a yell for bread,
and he cut them each a slice. He began eating his slowly, waiting for the kettle to boil.

How good the bread tasted. He studied the smooth, brown
upper crust and the thick under crust, white with flour. How
good it was. He ate thankfully and understood how men have
come to say grace.

The door opened. His mother came in, a bulging market bag
hanging from her hand. "Oh, Zecky, I'm so glad you're home.
I forgot potatoes—and to climb the stairs again. Hurry up, Zecky.
It's late already. And look what they did here!" She raised her
voice at the sight of the pots and pans and the trail of the
youngster with soaking rompers.

Ezekiel was about to protest. He had his own work to do.
But at the sight and sound of her anger at the children, he held
out his hand for the nickel and pennies.

On his way back he thought, Now I'll have to tell Ma what
I want the things for. There's so much to explain and nothing
may come of it. Ezekiel was afraid that if he told, somehow his
strength would ooze away. And he liked to think that in these
apparently aimless wanderings, he was working out an intricate

and beautiful design. He would simply tell his mother that he needed the soap and things, that he would bring them right back, and would explain afterwards.

He put the bag of potatoes on the washtub. His brothers, tears still in their eyes from the spanking, jumped about, shouting, "I wanna napple, I wanna napple." The bag fell to one side and out of its curves rolled two or three potatoes. At their dismal brown, the noise stopped. "Zecky, I haven't a match in the house," his mother began plaintively.

It would have been easy enough to borrow some next door, if the people had not moved out. The walk to his store would take him forty minutes. It would soon be dark, and what could he do there then? "What is the matter with you?" he shouted. "My whole day is taken up running around for you. Can't you tell me everything at one time?"

"Well, I forgot. Believe me, I have enough on my head. Am I playing? Don't you see I haven't got a minute's rest? And I have lived to have a son like you—a help! Not a penny does he bring in the house, but give him eat, give him clothes, and he bosses yet. A blessing on our heads! And when I ask him to run down for me a minute, when I am so tired I can't stand on my feet, look at the mouth he opens. Have you heard it?"

"All right, all right, I'll go, I'll go, only keep still."

"Go in the hell! Here." She counted three pennies out of her pocketbook and slapped them on the table. He picked them up and ran downstairs.

His mother thought, as she peeled the potatoes and they fell white and plump into the clear water, What is the matter with my head that I forget like that? He is right. Is it right to send a man to the grocery like a little boy? I must make him think himself a man with a man's work to do, and I keep treating him like a boy. Is it any wonder that he acts like he does?

* * *

It was too late to go to his store. In a little while it began to grow
dark. From the window, Ezekiel saw the peddlers taking their
places along the curb. Soon the sidewalks, and the gutters, too,
were crowded with working men and girls going home. The
peddlers shouted. Three or four pushcarts had gas-jets, now
flaring the twilight. The shop windows and electric signs lit up.
Ezekiel heard the purring of the sign below. It was night at last.
In the street, the peddlers shouted. Ezekiel heard the elevated
trains, the clanging streetcars, the impatient horns of the motor
trucks, the thousand feet and voices of the crowd at high tide.

The gas was lit in the kitchen. He saw his sisters moving
about. As Ezekiel went in, the light hurt his eyes.

His father was seated at the table and on a plate before him
were two potatoes, smoking hot. As he broke them up and
swallowed piece after piece, Saul kept opening his thick lips and
drawing in his breath to cool the lump of potato, his mouth
and throat. Like a fish, Ezekiel thought.

Ezekiel's sisters were bringing plates to the table and talking
to each other. "Cut bread," their mother shouted, bending over
the pot.

"You do it," Esther shouted at her sister, "don't you see I'm
setting the table?"

"And what am I doing, you dope?"

Their father banged the table with his fist so that the plates
and cutlery jumped. "Let it be still," he shouted in Yiddish.
"Enough noise all day in the shop. When I come home, I want
quiet."

They were silent. He fell to on the meat and potatoes heaped
upon his plate. The sisters made faces at each other. Sarah Yetta
served her daughters and son, darting angry glances at each.

When he had finished, Saul slouched back, his head sunk
forward, his eyes fixed in a stare. Ezekiel studied their yellow-
ish whites with specks of red and blue and the faded brown of

the pupils. The bald forehead, breaking out in a fine sweat, glistened under the gaslight. His cheeks and chin were covered with a brown and grey bristle.

A belch shook him. He got up slowly and walked to the sink, spat into it, and poured himself a glass of water. "Why don't we have water on the table?" he said crossly, and went into the bedroom.

They could hear the bed creak as he sat on it. And then the shoes hit the floor, one, two. The bed creaked again, and all was still.

Esther had put on her hat and with her little finger was smearing the red of the lipstick over her lips. "Where are you going?" Rebecca whispered in agony. "It's your turn to wash the dishes. It ain't fair, Ma, it ain't fair."

"I don't feel well tonight," Esther said, and turned on Ezekiel. "Why don't you do it? We work hard all day. You don't do nothing, why don't you do it? I'm not going to do it, let him do it." And she hurried out, closing the door behind her against argument and threat.

"Yes," Rebecca took up the attack, "we work hard all day. We got enough to do."

"Keep still, you'll wake up the children, you'll wake Papa up. I don't want him to do it. It isn't a man's work. I'll do it myself." And Sarah Yetta rose and began piling up the dishes.

"I don't want you to, Mamma," Rebecca said, "go away." And she began to carry the dishes to the sink. Her eyes overflowed. "But it ain't fair, Mamma, it ain't fair. It's Esther's turn tonight. And, anyway, Zecky ought to do it. He don't do nothing all day now. Why can't he do it, the big bum?" Ezekiel took his cap and went out.

The stoop was empty. If it were summer it would be crowded, and he thought of himself picking his way among those seated along the steps. Excuse me. There! He had stepped on someone's hand. He could feel the fingers numb between his shoe and the stone.

He crossed the Bowery and walked up Prince Street, through the Italian quarter. The street was quiet. A wall of red brick shut in the garden of a nunnery, all but an elm that managed to look over. Broadway, too, was quiet: just a man or a motor car, now and then, and a streetcar, almost empty. The side streets were black, except where the lamps lit up the shop signs and the silence.

At last he came to his store. The shine of the street lamps along the plate glass—the window seemed to him a pool in the desert of brick houses. He tried to look inside, but all was pitch dark.

Should he open the door and go in? To do what in the darkness? He took out the key. He would just try the lock.

He slipped the key into the keyhole and imagined himself a thief. He tried to turn the key gently. It would not budge. For a panic-stricken minute he pressed hard upon it, the bolt slid back with a loud noise, and the door was open. Then he turned the key back and tried the handle three or four times to make sure the door was locked.

His mother and sisters would still be up. The kitchen, in which he slept, would be crowded with their talk—to fall on his mind like handfuls of gravel on a pane of glass. He walked along the streets, imagining them canals and bathing in their silence.

He became impatient, wanted the night done with as soon as possible, thought of all the days he had wasted, and stretched out for the morrow. It was early, and the street in which he lived was still noisy.

He opened the door. Yes, his mother and Rebecca were seated in the glare of the gaslight, talking away. "Listen, I've got to go to bed early," he said, "so please go out." "What's the matter, you've got a job?" Rebecca sneered. They had long given up hope of any job for Ezekiel. What to do with him was a mountain in their midst, at which they each shied an angry or malicious or calmly earnest word, but the mountain stayed.

"Go on out now. Mamma, I've got to get up early. Go down to the stoop if you want to talk. Anyway, what are you staying cooped up here for?"

His mother went into the bedroom. "It's too early to go to bed," Rebecca said. "Only people who don't have to work go to bed now," and she slammed the door behind her.

Ezekiel ran after her into the hall to punch her. "Do you want to wake up Papa and the kids?" She screamed, and catching hold of the banisters, clattered downstairs.

His mother had brought out his quilts, sheet, and pillow. "Don't bother, Ma." He pushed the chairs together to make his bed on them.

She stood in the doorway. "What's a matter, Zecky? Don't you feel good? Does your head hurt?"

"I've got a lot of work tomorrow, and I want to go to bed early. I feel fine, Ma. Goodnight."

The light of the window across the airshaft covered him with a golden cloth. The distant noises of the street and the dim voices of the neighbors, his father's snoring, the faint noises that his mother made beyond the closed door as she undressed, fell silently into his calm spirit.

His steps became slow. In the daylight how drab his plans were.

He saw the sun large as it is, not small as it seems, and the earth, small as it is, not large as it seems. What men have done and what a man, if he were to meet a being of another planet, might boast of, seemed to him at that moment unimportant, as the earth itself in the heavens.

He was tired, as if his muscles were tired. If the grave were open, he would step in, to be out of the noise of the world and its lights, the great light and the lesser lights and the many tiny lights that man has made, to rest in the darkness, in the black of nothingness forever.

The wind blew the dust of the street into his face, blackening his nostrils, blew dust upon his lips. How should he escape? From how many windows and roofs to fall, before how many trains, cars, and motor cars to jump, how easy to walk into the Harlem River, the East River, the Hudson River, the Bay, the Sound, the sea at a hundred beaches.

Why should he? Surely he who cared so little for life could dare heights and distances—there to find, perhaps, nectar and ambrosia? So after all I am a romanticist, Ezekiel thought.

Now his wish to live ordered him into action. And like a good private, without further question, sure of no other value in the command but to make him forget himself, he came home quickly to do what he had planned.

Why should I keep it a secret, he thought, if it would give Ma a little courage about me? So he told her what he had done and wanted to do.

She looked at him doubtfully. She had heard too many of his plans and had seen them come to nothing. But she gave him what he asked for. "Bring them right back, soon as you are through." When the door closed behind him, she went to the window and said a little prayer.

Ezekiel turned the faucet of the sink in the back of the store. For a moment he was afraid that the water was shut off, but it splashed down with a cheerful noise. He took its presence as a good omen and imagined himself one of his ancestors who had just dug a well in the desert.

He filled the pail and set to work scrubbing the floor.

This was only covered with dust; it was no hard job to

make the floor fairly clean again. As he was kneeling over the scrubbing brush and the bubbling wash it left, he heard the door opened. The grocer looked on, smiling. "Hard at it, eh?"

It was a long time since he had seen approval in anybody's eyes and a stranger's at that. Ezekiel worked with a will. It was pleasant to have a job after his long idleness, pleasant to move his muscles, pleasant to make the dirty floor clean, the dirty window shine, to rub the woodwork clean of dust, and to know, when all was done, he would be the master.

At last he was through. An empty box had been left in the store, and he stood this up for a seat. He washed his hands and waved them in the air until they were dry. Then he took out of his pocket the piece of rye bread he had brought with him, and seated on the box ate slowly, gazing with satisfaction at the wet floor and bright window.

He was tired; his knees ached, and his arms ached. Though he had started briskly enough, when he had gone a little way, he slowed up, and the walk home never seemed as long and tedious and the stairs as troublesome. He placed his bundle on the washtub and felt that he could do no more that day.

He walked to the front room and sat in the armchair. He thought of his shop, the clean floor on which the water was drying and the bright window. He remembered how, too young to walk, he was crawling up a dark flight of stairs. Upon the upper landing the sunlight shone through a window.

His mother came gently into the room. She smiled and said, "You are not used to that work. Lie down a little." She wiped an apple in her apron until the red skin shone and left it on the arm of the chair.

He held the apple to his nose. He had read of a dying rabbi who kept smelling at an apple for the strength to speak his last words. Bright and red, it was the earth upon which the sun shone. It seemed to Ezekiel that the world was good and every breath he drew precious. His body was tired, but his heart fresh and joyful.

When he woke, it was dusk. He went to the window. The street lamps were lit. He could see a large white star in the sky.

After supper, when the table was cleared, the girls and his mother went out. He took some paper, pen and ink, and the ruler, and set himself to making two signs. The first read, *If you are interested in books, come in and let's have a chat. Ezekiel Rubinov*; the second, *Have you heard of J. P. Irvine? Let me read you one of his poems. Ezekiel Rubinov.*

He made a horn of paper and poured in a little flour. He searched among his books for those from which to read passages that moved him. Then he took a rag and rubbed his shoes clean. He rummaged for the clothes brush in the old trunk in which his sisters kept their things and brushed away until he felt clean and respectable. The effect on his clothes, though, was not particularly noticeable.

His nap had left him wide awake. He walked along the brightly lit streets, watching the girls that passed, but they barely glanced at him. He came out of the bright streets of the East Side into Lafayette Place; he walked up the dark blocks of Fourth Avenue into Fourteenth Street.

Two girls, one grown fat and matronly, leered at him. Their ugliness was like a bad smell, and he hurried away. A tall Irish girl hurried along Fourth Avenue. She seemed the most beautiful woman he had ever seen. A tall sailor, his face bright red, caught her by the arm. She tried to shake him off. "Hey, don't you remember me? Don't you remember that night at Charley's?" He grinned. She looked at him and laughed. He put his arm through hers, and they were off. Ezekiel walked on; the night became tedious, and he went home.

In the morning, to begin with, he picked one of the new publishers. They would be more responsive than old, established firms. The address was in a new building, whose glistening tower rose thirty stories above the street.

Hesitating, Ezekiel was whirled through the revolving door into the marble lobby, into an elevator, up into a hall, and deposited in the outer office, feeling like an express package, battered in transit, with a wrapper dirty and a little torn.

A woman lifted a drawn, yellow face from above a typewriter. "Well?"

"I want to make some arrangement about handling your books. You see, I have a store." The large oriental rug he stood on glowed. He lifted his eyes to the walls to see signed photographs of writers newly famous. His assurance—only a coating —was now dissolved, and he knew himself unpleasant to the taste of the sane inhabitants of this elegance. He felt as he imagined his ancestors might have when they were making sacrifices to bone-eyed idols, before they knew the true God, Who understands and is merciful. "I have no money, but I have a shop, and should like to have your books on sale. Of course, what I'll sell I'll pay for out of the money I'll get in; what I don't sell you'll have back."

The smile with which she had greeted him had long before crept back between the crack of her lips. The thought of how her typing had been needlessly interrupted and of how much she had still to do, hardened her face. "Miss Tyler," she turned to a girl of twenty-three-or-four, who was hovering about, "will you please take care of the office?"

Miss Tyler had curly hair and bright eyes and a sweet, well-formed mouth, as if it had tasted much good poetry—and round shoulders, as if she read too much. She looked at Ezekiel over her shoulder as she went to put some papers in a drawer, with so merry a glance, so good-natured and friendly, that he thought it the most natural thing in the world for him to say, Won't you come to see me in my store sometime? And he was just about to do so when the ogress came back.

"Mr. Langdell is busy and can't see you just now." She kept taking in his appearance, as if she were astounded at that in their office and at his request from one in such clothes.

Surely what he had asked for was not utterly foolish. They could not lose. But he would lose his time if nothing sold. He smiled at the thought that his time had become an asset.

He was in the elevator and out in the street. After all, he was a customer. What fools to treat him like that. Suppose his store became large and prosperous someday? Then they would be all smiles and bows.

But going there had been worthwhile, if only to see Miss Tyler. That was decidedly worthwhile. If he hadn't gone into this enterprise, he would have missed her. He had taken booty in that office, after all.

He went to another address on his list. The outer office here was bright with sunshine. There were no lamps, no oriental carpet, but linoleum, partitions varnished yellow, and plain chairs.

The boy came back. "Mr. Butler will see you. The gentleman at that desk."

Mr. Butler motioned Ezekiel to a seat and looked at him casually. Ezekiel stated his business, but this time thought it discreet to say nothing about having no money. "I am sorry," Mr. Butler said, "but it is against the rule of the house to send books on consignment." He made a slight deprecating wave with his right hand.

"But what have you to lose?" Ezekiel began.

Mr. Butler looked impatiently at the papers on his desk. Ezekiel sat on. Mr. Butler took up his pen.

"Perhaps you can tell me the name of a publisher"—Mr. Butler looked up as if surprised to find Ezekiel still there—"who would," Ezekiel concluded lamely.

"I am sorry, but—" he shook his head. "Good-day." Mr. Butler allowed a little smile to move his lips. In a second it was gone, and he had turned from Ezekiel.

Ezekiel had no wish to face anyone else. He turned into Fifth Avenue, drifted with the crowd, and went on to Washington Square. He had no place to go and nothing to do.

He went down Broadway until he came to Chambers Street. He had not walked across Brooklyn Bridge since he was a boy. He made his way through the passage under the elevated trains, across the tracks of the street-cars, through the yellow darkness with its dim electric lights, the clanging of gongs, and the screech of wheels as the trolleys turned in the loops.

He was glad to find himself on the bridge, the tenements and office buildings behind him, his face towards the sky. Soon the roadway changed to slats of wood, springy under his feet after so many miles of asphalt. Ezekiel was pleased, too, after the even curves of gutters and the straight lines of pavements and houses to see the free glitter of the water. He was now in the rhythm of walking, that sober dance which despite all the dances man knows, he dances most.

Soon the bridge sloped to Brooklyn. Should he go on? He remembered the dingy streets in which the bridge ended—and faced the towers New York has thrown up, climbing on steel and granite from its narrow island into the illimitable sky. Ezekiel remembered reading in the newspapers, when a child, that the Singer Building was to be built, and he had heard the riveters on many others. He saw in those towers, already grown so familiar, the beginning of a myth: men would confuse them, perhaps, with those of Camelot, and through the millennia would look back at them with eager eyes.

As he walked between the steel ropes hanging in nets from the cables of the bridge, it seemed to him that—hundreds of feet wide and high—the mesh was about to close upon him. He remembered the song he used to sing, but now it was not Brooklyn Bridge that was falling down, it was Ezekiel Rubinov.

He could go home, of course. But he did not want to face his mother just yet. He walked on, beyond Twenty-third Street, aimlessly. He was so tired he could only shuffle along. If he had any place to go, but to spend the day like this until evening, and to spend day after day like this, week after week...

He remembered how often he had feared death, how it had seemed to him that he would never tire of living—how old men and women cling to life, though they ail and live only to know trouble after trouble, yet their hunger for life becomes avidity. But now he was tired of the sky and the monotonous streets, the men and women that passed.

He entered upon his familiar despondency, as when he saw clouds gathering and knew that it would rain, and that the rain, too, would pass, but in the meantime bowed his head to the cold, damp wind. When this mood came upon Ezekiel at other times, a brisk walk would cure it. Now at the thought of walking when he was so tired because of walking, he smiled.

As he walked along, he saw that he was near the address of one of the smaller publishers. Not to see him—nor to face anyone, for that matter—but to give his own wandering some direction, he walked to the number. Then it occurred to him to go up and talk to this publisher, too. He had no hope of anything, but it would be amusing to try, and help pass the time.

He was no longer Ezekiel Rubinov. Ezekiel Rubinov was a puppet whose strings he pulled. And this puppet would enter the office and face the slight surprise behind the door of a new room. The puppet would make a little speech. It would be a scene from a little comedy that he would start, and the comedy would then act itself without anymore trouble on his part than to act Ezekiel Rubinov. He was so sure of a refusal that he was unconcerned: he remembered a line of James Thomson's *The City of Dreadful Night*, "No hope can have no fear."

At the last turn of a corridor, he entered the office. From where he stood at the low railing, he could see a boy lounging in a sort of cubbyhole, stacked with books, a girl at a desk near the railing, and a man at a desk near the only window.

The man looked up as Ezekiel came in, and went back to his dreaming. Then he rose as if to make a show of decent activity and walked slowly to a file. He walked with a stoop, and after he had found a letter, returned with it to the desk and sat down heavily. Ezekiel thought, He acts well, quite naturally. It was Ezekiel's cue now. He bowed to the girl. "May I see Mr. Diamond?"

Ezekiel read his lips. "Just a minute." She reported, "Mr. Diamond will see you in just a minute. Won't you have a seat?" and she returned to her desk.

Ezekiel watched her nimble fingers. She was unconcerned at the heap of circulars and the pile of envelopes that moved downward slowly. He was reminded of a sage who said, "If you have much that is unpleasant to do, set about it quietly; soon it will be done." How fortunate he was: he had found beauty in the first publisher's office and wisdom in this.

The girl interrupted the soliloquy. "Mr. Diamond will see you now."

Ezekiel had difficulty in rising. The muscles of his legs had stiffened. He had no doubt that the spectators would think him merely clumsy. However, these were only his fellow actors, and they were paying him no attention.

There was a chair near Mr. Diamond, and unbidden, Ezekiel

sat down slowly. He even dared cross his legs and lean back a little. Mr. Diamond looked up. Ezekiel waited a second or two before speaking. He was too tired and had almost forgotten his lines.

"I have just rented a store in Greenwich Village," he managed to say, and was glad to hear his voice so calm. "Though, perhaps, *rented* is not right, because I have no rent to pay, unless I make good. I should like to stock the store with books. The store is not large, and, besides, it will be wholly unpretentious, so that I shall not need many books at first. But I have no money, none whatever. However, I offer you a place in which to display as many books as you wish, a man to do his best to sell them, and who will keep them as clean as they are in your own stock-rooms." Ezekiel thought the plural a diplomatic touch. "Whatever I sell will be paid for as soon as I sell them."

Mr. Diamond said nothing, and Ezekiel went on. "Perhaps you would like to know something about me. I should like to build up a business of my own, and am convinced that to treat everyone justly is the quickest way. This is bred in my bones. As you know, my ancestors were great readers of the Bible; some, perhaps, helped write it." Ezekiel thought it fun to poke a rocket into Mr. Diamond's face, discharge a few colored stars across the night, and step back, a Whistler, to watch the effect. But Mr. Diamond was lost in his own thoughts.

Ezekiel went on. "You can lose nothing but a little trouble to your help, and will gain at least a few sales and, perhaps, a good account." He remembered that that argument had worked with the grocer, and it still seemed to have a cutting edge.

Ezekiel waited for an answer and was encouraged to think that Mr. Diamond was considering the matter, because he did not answer right off. Mr. Diamond was thinking of some notes he had to meet.

He had begun as a publisher of translations from the French.

To these he added translations from the Swedish, Russian, Italian, and Polish. The books were good, the translations good enough, well printed and bound, but most of them sold little and slowly, some not at all, and only four or five well—but nothing to what other publishers sold of ordinary books. And, finally, Mr. Diamond's assets had dwindled until they were books packed away on his shelves and the shelves of his binders, dead stock, while printers' bills and binders' bills and bills for advertising were very much alive, and even when satisfied by a payment on account, came bouncing back for more.

If only he could say good-by forever to his office, to his ugly stenographer and all his creditors. And why had he let this boy in to pester him?

Mr. Diamond came out of his lethargy. What did it matter? He would get only ten cents each for his books from dealers, and at that would only sell a few hundred; he could get only two or three cents each for the lot. And unless he raised some money, God knew how, the creditors would get them, anyway.

What did it matter if this fellow stole a few books: they were worth little enough. And then he might sell some and pay for some. The sun came out and shone upon both.

"All right," said Mr. Diamond. "Here is my catalogue. Take it home and make out the list of books you want." He was anxious to slide back into his muddy thoughts, but Ezekiel did not dare climb that mountain again, now that hope had made him dizzy.

"Can't we settle it now?" Ezekiel answered. "I should like to open up as soon as possible—tomorrow night, if possible."

He remembered that though the store had a gas-lamp, he had no money for a deposit; and they would not turn on the gas before they had that. Ezekiel brushed away the thought like a fly and ran through the catalogue. His eyes lit up as he read name after name dear to him. "What excellent books you have!"

Mr. Diamond brightened. "If they were not so good, they might sell." He was sorry he had said that. But Ezekiel felt that what he had said was just right: it had pleased Mr. Diamond and showed that he understood the value of Mr. Diamond's books.

But the list was not large. He would not have much variety. Well, that couldn't be helped. "I should like twenty-five each of these titles: that would enable me to display each properly. And have you any posters or window displays?"

Mr. Diamond had not. He looked through the titles Ezekiel had checked. Of some he had sold perhaps a bare dozen that year. Mr. Diamond took out his pencil and counted the titles. About forty.

Why this was almost fifteen hundred dollars' worth of books at list prices. Ridiculous! To a chap who walked in from the street! But suppose the books could be closed out at twenty-five cents each: that would be a good price. He had been offered only ten cents each for small lots. At twenty-five cents that would be two hundred and fifty dollars for the thousand. Wasn't that their real value at most? Suppose he got that out of Ezekiel and Ezekiel decamped with the rest, wouldn't that be a good price? Mr. Diamond went through the figures again—his failures had intimidated him: whatever he did was wrong.

Ezekiel, too, was afraid of the figures he had conjured up. He was about to cut down the number of books to ten each, perhaps five. But it would be wiser to wait until the other spoke. And Mr. Diamond said, "All right, you'll have them. What's the address?"

Ezekiel wrote his name and address slowly and in a large hand. He read the address twice before handing it to Mr. Diamond to make sure there was no mistake. This was the time to rise, to thank Mr. Diamond, and to say good-by.

He walked along the street, the wind flapping the large banner he imagined that he carried. Then doubts like crows came out of the blue sky and followed him. Suppose Mr. Diamond went down to the store to see who this Ezekiel Rubinov was, and found it bare of shelving, of even table and chairs, would he send the books, or if they were sent, would he not take them back? And what should be done about lights? Most of the business would be in the evening and could he sell books in the dark? There were still other doubts he could not name; but they gathered into a great cloud and he knew it as hunger.

To pass the time he wondered what he would do if he had a nickel. He might buy a cup of coffee, or a bar of chocolate, or a box of crackers, or a roll and two penny packages of chocolate, or an apple and a roll, or a loaf of bread. It was ridiculous to be in want of just a nickel in the streets of New York.

When he was a boy, he sometimes found a penny—once a dime—in the streets. Surely there were hundreds and hundreds of dollars in change lying that moment along the miles of sidewalks and in the gutters. If he were to devote himself to looking for it, he might make a good living and, certainly, it was not as unpleasant as some work. He would be in the open air, at least.

If a coin should drop on the sidewalk, it would be quickly picked up. But if money fell out of men's pockets as they hurried across the street, Ezekiel reasoned, it would roll into the gutters. The street cleaners, most likely, picked up everything there: between their rounds was his chance. He saw himself a savage hunting for a root he knew of to stop his hunger. If there was woodcraft, Ezekiel thought, he was master of a new science, citycraft.

He began to search at once, walking along the curb, his eyes in the gutter. Now and then he could not help stepping off and so often an automobile or truck rushed close by, he realized the business was not without its dangers. After only a block and a half he found a quarter. There it was, shiny in the newly swept gutter, the marks of the street-cleaner's broom across it. He picked it up and looked about.

The quarter was worn smooth, and he let it clink on the sidewalk to make sure it was not counterfeit. He was too impatient now for anything but a restaurant. At an Automat, five or six blocks down, he changed it into real nickels, and smiled at the thought that the cashier might say, This quarter is no good: "'tis of the unsubstantial fabric of a dream."

This was going to be a feast and for that he would wash his hands carefully. Though he was so hungry, now that he would be fed, he took his time. He delighted in the cool water and the rough clean paper towels. Then he made the round of the little compartments and studied through the thick glass the little pots of dark brown beans, the meat pies—the brown crust curling away from the thick dishes—the dishes of macaroni with yellow nuggets of melted cheese, the pompous apple dumplings in ermine of vanilla sauce, then the sandwiches: rows bright with sliced tomatoes and green lettuce, with the red of smoked meats, or the pastel tints of cheese.

Why spend anything? He was going home. He would weaken himself not only by having less, but in that he yielded. Still, to spend one nickel would not be extravagant, and he ought to celebrate.

Coffee streamed into his cup. He lowered his head to breathe its fragrance. It seemed to him that he was carrying a small pot of earth from which the steam, a fragrant bush, grew. The grains of sugar in the heaping teaspoonful glittered. They sank into the coffee, and their light became sweetness. He drank slowly.

It warmed and cheered him. The lights of the ceiling shone into the core of his being. He thought of himself as a soldier, resting from battle, or a sailor, during a lull in the storm, drinking hot coffee.

He walked for a block or two before he remembered to
look along the gutter. For a mile he found nothing. A policeman eyed him. At last he picked up a dime. It was no longer
precious, and he looked no more.

In the Italian quarter he joined a crowd before a florist's shop.
Out came the picture of a saint on the shoulders of bare-headed
men, the frame stuck over with pink paper roses and green
dollar bills. The brass band in the middle of the street struck
up a lively air, most of the men in the crowd took off their hats,
the open windows of the tenements were jammed with women
and children. First went the band, then the sacred picture with
a guard of children in Sunday clothes, their tall yellow candles
burning strangely in the sunlight, then a red banner and the
men of its society.

The procession turned into a street hung with arches of
colored electric bulbs and made its way between the pushcarts
and crowd until it reached a little red church.

There the band played louder than ever, a priest came to
the porch to welcome the picture, and it was brought inside;
the worshippers and their lighted candles followed. Women
from neighboring houses, covering their heads with black
shawls, hurried to join them.

Ezekiel waited in the street. As they came down the steps,
the men who carried the picture were sweating under the
heavy frame. He studied their stolid faces. The priest was left
on the steps. Still a young man, his fat belly showed under the
cassock; his ruddy face with its high broad forehead was proud
and intelligent.

The procession was on its way back. As he kept his hands
raised blessing it, the priest lifted his eyes to a window across
the street. Ezekiel followed his glance and saw over a flower-

box a face as intelligent as the priest's, but it was thin; the man had long black hair, and his lips were curled in a broad smile. Beside him stood a woman and her ruddy, pretty face was also wreathed in smiles. The priest turned to the procession and its crowd, now halfway up the block, and flung his hands down as if in disgust. He smiled up to the smiling man and woman.

The comedy over, Ezekiel walked the gallery of the push-carts, examining the exhibits: the peaceful colors of vegetables or a cart bright with oranges. When he came to a Carnegie library, he went in out of habit. It seemed to him a long time since he had been in such a room. He took an anthology from the shelf and read a page here and there. The lights were lit and still he read on.

When he was back in the street it was night. He was cold and faint with hunger. He opened the door and found them all about the table. As he ate his eyes closed for weariness. He would have gone to sleep as soon as dinner was over, but the dishes had to be washed and wiped and put away, and the room would be noisy and lighted for a long time.

It was too cold to sleep on the roof. He spread his blanket at the end of the hall: they lived on the top floor, and no one would be going to the roof now. He took off his shoes and put them alongside; untied his necktie and stuffed it into his pocket, and unbuttoned the collar of his shirt. Surely a neck-tie, he thought, is Jeremiah's halter that a man ties about his neck each day as a symbol of his life.

How good to rest. The gas-jet in the hall on the floor below was lit: how pleasant to lie in the darkness and see the light streaming up between the banisters. He heard a squabble in his home. It did not matter: he was outside. Soon the oil of sleep pouring over him drowned his mind.

Something had touched his face. It was pitch dark: after ten o'clock the light downstairs was out. He caught up the blanket to go into the house. Something soft fell on the floor and scampered away, its nails faintly clicking. Too light for a dog or cat and too heavy for a mouse. A rat! He shivered and felt his upper lip curl in disgust.

It was cold in the kitchen, too. It was too early in the season to make the stove; for it was only cold late at night when everyone was or ought to be asleep and covered. He was stiff and knocked into a chair. He felt about in the dark, put the chairs together, undressed, then spread the blanket on the seats and wrapping himself in it, with his arm for a pillow, fell asleep.

He was walking in a narrow street, and after a while knew it as the stable street through which he went to kindergarten. The large doors of the stables were open, for it was May. In the dark interiors he could sometimes see a man polishing a carriage or leading a horse with noisy hoofs up an incline. The stench of the stables burned his nostrils, but in his hand was a spray of lilacs. This was for his teacher. He bent over to smell the lilacs only. A cluster touched his face. It was like the muzzle of the rat, and he woke with a start.

The sky was grey. The dawn lit up the kitchen and he was wide awake (because he had gone to sleep so early the night before). He hurried to dress and wash and be out under that strange sky before it was day.

No one was in the street but the milkman. Lights were shining in the groceries: he could see the grocers and their sleepy boys filling paper bags with rolls, the warm smell of which filtered through the open doors.

Ezekiel took deep breaths of the cold air. Even these streets were quiet now. His sleep had become a long pleasant dream.

In the bright morning he looked eagerly at the houses, at each horse and milk wagon—some had the lantern hung from the axle still burning—and at each vivid laborer that passed.

More and more people were in the streets, until Ezekiel, thinking of Wordsworth, found himself in the light of common day.

He felt for the four nickels in his pocket. The silver of the thin dime was an unexpected pleasure: he had not thought of it, and it was as if he had just found it. He would not have to go home for breakfast; and this taste of freedom was so dear to him, he made up his mind to husband every cent he could to be free.

He reached the Automat where he had had coffee the afternoon before. Now a row of compartments showed halves of melons, gaudy reddish yellows, and at the steam table were strips of bacon, dark against a huge dish of scrambled eggs. He had coffee and the modest yellow of three corn muffins, and was satisfied.

He had planned to ask the grocer for empty boxes and set them together as a table. This would have to do for fixtures, except two boxes he would use to sit on, until he had money to spend on shelving and a real table and chairs. He had better wait, though, until the shipment of books came before asking for the boxes.

There were other publishers he was now eager to see, but the delivery man from Diamond's must not find the door closed. Ezekiel took two of his own books and placed them as a seat on the cold stone of the step.

He turned to the poem James of Scotland wrote when a prisoner in the Tower of London. The *Kingis Quair* was fresh and pleasant in the early morning: the garden, trees and flowers, and birds singing, and the three ladies with their fresh fair faces walking along the path beside the hedge. He read on along the even rise and fall of the rich rhyme, until a shadow covered the page.

He looked up at a girl, a twinkle in her blue eyes the brighter for her dark skin.

"Are you the owner?"

"Yes," he said.

"Well, what have you for sale?" And she looked into the empty store with a mischievous smile.

"Won't you come in and see?" he said gravely, picking up the two books in the way. The King sang on and Ezekiel felt as merry, though he kept his face as grave as the Barmecide in the *Arabian Nights*. She hesitated and then crossed the threshold.

"Here," he said, pointing to the blank wall, "are paintings from Japan. If I were an artist, I would go to Tokyo, not to Paris. Look," and remembering an exhibit he had seen several times, "here is a catfish turning in the water. The motion of all the waters of earth is here; here are all the ripples, currents, waves, and tides; here is the horror of muddy depths of ponds, lakes, and rivers, and of the green depths of the sea, the horror of cold-blooded fish and crawling things.

"Here is a white cat under a spray of white flowers. The cat looks up at us: its body bulges, the green eyes burn among the dull whites of fur and flowers. Here are cranes on a frosty morning. The two birds, hunched up, shiver. See, about the soft, blurred white of their bodies the reeds in broad curves— grey reeds, dull green reeds, dull brown and red," and Ezekiel pointed to some cracks in the wall. "And here is a sparrow flattened against a branch for warmth. From the brown twigs hang a few brown leaves, swayed to one side by the wind. See, the polished blue-white sky of winter."

Ezekiel turned from the wall. They had reached the back of the store. "As you see, there are more, better ones, but you are tired. I'll show you the rest another time."

"I'm not tired at all. Please go on."

"I've lots besides Japanese paintings. Here is something from the Chinese. Hold one end of the scroll, please. Now," and Ezekiel made believe he was unrolling it, "look at this prairie fire. What a sweep of flames! See the little blackened skeletons of trees left behind. The flames are coming down on this field of large feathery stalks of grass. Here is a gazelle in front of the flames, its head lifted in agony. Here is the white tail of another, diving into the grass. The sky in back is golden with fire, in front black with smoke." He waved the scroll aside without troubling to roll it up.

She stood quite close to him. It seemed easy enough to put his arm about her and say, "Here's a kiss for breakfast," and he was sure she would not mind. But he had never kissed a woman and was timid. Besides, that Chinese scroll with its flames—the only one he could think of at the moment—might have put her out of the mood for kisses.

"I am going to open a bookshop," he said simply, "and I hope when the books come, you'll visit us."

"I'd be glad to," she said. "I see you have a few books."

"These are not for sale: they are mine." As he bent to show them, he uncovered the signs he meant to place on the window. "What do you think of these? I can't afford to have the window lettered just now. I mean to paste these up instead."

She took them from his hand. "Who is J. P. Irvine?"

"I don't think many know of him. I have never read of him anywhere, nor anything of his except in John Burrough's anthology. What do you think of this at the end of his poem 'Indian Summer'?

'The sharp staccato barking of a squirrel,
            A dropping nut, and all again is still.'

Or this from 'An August Afternoon on the Farm'?

'So dragged the day, but when the dusk grew deep
   The stagnant heat increased; we lit no light,
But sat out-doors, too faint and sick for sleep.'"

After a minute she said, "Very good." But Ezekiel could see
that her eyes were faraway and the words mechanical. She
shook her head slightly as if to rouse herself. "Thank you so
much. I write verse myself and some day I'll come in and let you
read mine." As if this could only be followed by a retreat, she
added hurriedly, "I'll be late uptown," and gave him her hand.

He sat down on the steps. At noon he thought of buying a
box of crackers at the landlord's but was afraid of questions,
for he could still show nothing but the cleaning he himself had
given the place. He scrawled a sign, "Back in two minutes," stuck
it on the door, and left in a fever for fear the delivery man
should come while he was out. It seemed to him many blocks
before he found a grocery, and he ran all the way back, half
expecting to see someone waiting in front of the store.

The crackers filled his mouth with dust, but he chewed away
resolutely until he had eaten all. He made a cup of his hands:
the water from the faucet, even though he let it run a long time,
had tiny flakes of black in it. He decided not to drink. After a
while his thirst would pass, as it often did, just like hunger and
cold. The body, he had found, makes its need known and after
a while, unanswered, concludes its master cannot satisfy it,
though he would, or is busy, and courteously becomes silent.

He wondered at the body's wisdom that is not of the mind
and how each of the body's parts lives its own life. He saw himself a composite, his life a number of particles, like the mist—
returning to air and water as the weather changes. Images, like
frost on a window-pane, grew out of each other in his mind—to
melt away.

The afternoon passed slowly. No one came in, and of those

who passed, none gave the shop more than a glance. The books did not come.

How pleasantly the day had begun and how it was ending, quietly and sad, as the end of most men and women, he thought: not the "misery and madness" Wordsworth tells of as the end of poets—"we poets whose lives begin in gladness"—but such an end as Wordsworth's, plenty of money, enough milk for tea, parted from the friends of his youth, writing on and on—everything said long before, his sister's mind gone and only her smile still the same, and the sunlight, yes, even "the light of common day" fading out of the sky, little done and neither strength nor light nor time in which to do more.

Ezekiel felt his own disappointment lost in the ocean of human sorrow surging over the tallest buildings. He wondered if men, like coral, would be able to build on their own skeletons dry land at last.

He waited on until it was black night. He locked the door and was walking away, when it struck him, since bookshops were often open at night, a delivery might be made later. He turned back and waited in the darkness. He wondered should Diamond's man come, if it were not better to have the store closed and dark than open and dark; if it would have betrayed an impatience disquieting to Mr. Diamond to have telephoned that the books had not come, or whether it showed a disquieting indifference not to have telephoned.

The kitchen was empty except for his mother. As Sarah Yetta stood there, the gas lit up her wrinkled forehead. "Where were you? I was so worried."

"I was waiting for some books to come."

She lit the gas under the pot. "Where did you have breakfast? What did you eat all day?" She looked at him anxiously.

"Oh, I bought breakfast and lunch."

"Where did you get money?"

"I found it."

Was her son a thief? She looked at him with wide open eyes and pursed lips. He smiled and looked calmly into her eyes.

"I found thirty-five cents in the gutter and bought breakfast and lunch. This is left." He showed her the dime and nickel, as if that proved how he got them.

He remembered his thirst and drank a glass of water—a new and delightful drink. So, when I was nearly run over at a crossing, he thought, realizing how the ordinary becomes dear, I took a deep breath and found the air sweet.

His mother looked at him sadly. If the books had come, he would have had something to tell her; as it was, he ate and said nothing. When he was through, he rose and took the dish to the sink.

"Don't bother," she said and pushed him away. "I'll wash it. But tell me, Zecky, why did you stay in the store? I want to know everything."

She would have liked to pour out her love for her son in a long psalm of blessing and counsel, such as she heard in synagogue when a girl, but her tongue, fluent enough to scold and bargain, was now stiff. Her husband spoke little and had taken to grunts and gestures, their tongues grown coarse as their hands and faces.

Ezekiel went to the store next morning as calmly as a distant ancestor might have led his sheep to search for pasture. He did not know that there would be pasture, but he had found pasture before—"hitherto hath the Lord helped us"—and he looked about securely. Ezekiel had hardly unlocked the door, set it wide open and himself to reading, before a burly truckman was on the threshold. "This for you?" he asked, and showed a receipt.

"Yes."

He carried in bundle after bundle. It was all in the day's work for him, but to Ezekiel he was Aladdin's slave.

Ezekiel untied the knots and put aside for his own use the cord and wrapping paper. And there, on sheets of wrapping paper to keep them clean, stack on stack of books in rich jackets of many colors! Like huge fungi, Ezekiel thought. Suddenly grown out of the floor.

"Good morning," he said to the grocer, and in a voice he tried to keep matter-of-fact, "my books are beginning to come in. Can you lend me boxes and boards?"

"I have no boards." The grocer added, "Some boxes in the cellar." He struggled between reluctance, after watching the pennies for two decades, to give anything for nothing and the thought that by helping Ezekiel he was himself nearer the rent. "I passed the store last night and it was dark."

"There was no use opening up until the books came."

The grocer went outside and unlocked the cellar. Ezekiel lifted the iron doors and went down. He saw a heap of empty boxes, all kinds, small boxes of thick wood, large boxes with weak slats for sides. "Pile up on the sidewalk," the grocer called down, "what you think you want, and I'll look them over."

From the days when he had made himself a wagon, Ezekiel remembered that soap boxes were best, and sure enough they were the strongest of the large boxes. He searched until he had dragged out eighteen. There were more, but he was afraid to strain the grocer's good-will.

"They are worth a dime each," he said, when Ezekiel had the eighteen upstairs. "All right, I'll keep an eye on them until you carry them around. I suppose you're going to paint them: that won't look so bad."

"Yes, I'll paint them," Ezekiel answered, and added to himself, "when I get the money."

He put the boxes against the side walls, long side down, nine on each side, three and three, three high. The window ledge would do for a seat. He had fifteen cents to buy candles. Well, he would not sell many books at night until he could use the lamp. He made a paste of the flour he had brought from home and putting a little in each corner of the signs, stuck them on the window. Then he ranged the books, one of each title, along the two lower shelves—he did not use the top—until the shelves were filled; the rest he stacked in the bottom boxes. Of the two titles he liked best he placed some books in the window, and was ready for business.

A man walked in when Ezekiel had given up hope of customers until the afternoon. He examined the shelving. Ezekiel was glad he had pasted wrapping paper over the ends of the boxes to hide the soap legend.

"It's going to be cold here—just a cellar. No stove?"

"Not yet."

"And it's hot in summer. Never rent a store without a back door—can't air the place. Well, I'm not much for books: the newspaper's good enough for me. Just dropped in to look around. Good luck, my boy."

In an hour an old woman clambered down the steps to ask if he had Hallowe'en cards. Where could she get them? Ezekiel was not sure, but perhaps the stationery next block—and she climbed up the stairs, grumbling.

Then, as always when he least looked for it, a young man bustled in, ran his eyes over the shelves, said, "You haven't much to choose from, have you?" and took three books.

Ezekiel had used too much paper and he unwrapped the clumsy package and tore the sheet in half. Now there was too little paper and the books showed.

"That'll do. How much?"

"Six dollars."

The young man took a billfold from his pocket, spread out a sheaf of new bills, chose a five-dollar bill and a one-dollar bill and handed them to Ezekiel. He picked up the package and took the three steps at a bound. Ezekiel had not had time to thank him. Here he was with six dollars, no, with flocks of sheep and goats, herds of camels and asses, men servants and maid servants, rich as Abraham.

Others came in. Ezekiel remembered that he had not lunched, but did not care. Towards evening, he locked the door for a few minutes—it struck him that this was the first time he had reason to—and ran around to his landlord to buy half a dozen candles.

"Haven't you gas yet?"

"No, but I think I'll have tomorrow."

"You should have seen to that first. How are things?"

"Not so bad," and Ezekiel showed him the ten dollars he had taken in. "I think I'll be able to pay you an installment on your rent before the week is over."

The grocer became genial. He had been willing to lease the store rent-free for two months. "There's no hurry. I can wait another week. Better fix the place up a little."

Ezekiel saw the sky red in the west. He turned unwillingly to the store, and as he went down the steps into the dark, went into a prison cell he himself had built.

The ceiling of the shop was closing in on him. He would have to lower his head, bow, bend his shoulders, stoop, bend his knees. It was useless: he would be crushed at last.

The air of the shop was damp and stale in his nostrils. He lit the candles and stuck them on the boxes. His triumph had died: these were the funeral lights.

* * *

It was a warm, clear night. People drifted into the shop. They bantered him; and he joked too, of course, but the gas would be on tomorrow, this would be here, that there. They were just curious, strangers curious about the neighborhood, neighbors curious about the shop, but a few bought—more to oblige than to read—and he added to his money. It was pleasant to feel in his pocket the thickness of the bills, a charm against faintness. He stroked them, and they crackled in reply.

How foolish—bad for business, too—to be so faint! When a decent-looking man and his wife were in the shop, he asked them to mind it for a minute or two, while he went to buy a sandwich. He hurried out before they could answer; it was like leaving a baby on their hands, he thought, and smiled.

He was afraid that he would faint before he reached the store. If he hurried, he might faint from the exertion, slight as it was. The store was a block away, and he became aware that it was hundreds and hundreds of steps away. But he reached it, and the good smell of the place, the smell of meats and pickles and cakes and cheese, the food in naked reds and whites, or wrapped in silver tinfoil, and the brightly colored boxes of crackers revived him.

"Two cheese sandwiches—Swiss." The man cut them deftly and wrapped them up. Ezekiel picked an apple from the box and smelled it. He could barely wait to be out in the street.

Ezekiel unfolded the paper and rammed half a sandwich into his mouth. Then he gobbled the apple in three bites, core, stem, and all. The seeds slipped about in his mouth until they were chewed up. He was still hungry but no longer faint.

The somewhat bewildered couple were wondering whether to leave. He apologized. He was now ready for more customers, but none came. The candles were almost gone, and he closed the store.

It was morning and it was evening, the first day. Ezekiel had a vague recollection that he had been through such a day before. It must have been when he was little and played store selling pieces of paper for pins.

His brain was so busy he did not notice the streets. Yes, first the gas, then he would buy a table in a used furniture store he knew of near the Bowery, then chairs, perhaps a bench, then a can of olive green paint and a brush. He must make a payment to Diamond and one to the grocer—he would show him the liberality of a Jew. And then for himself, shoes and clothes.

The day was good, but perhaps first days are. People come in out of curiosity, still hunting, find the ordinary, and never come again.

His mother would be waiting. She was worried, perhaps, now that she had least cause to worry. He could bring her a gift whom he knew only as giving. Was the money his? Was it not Diamond's and the grocer's? Yes, but she too was a creditor. He bought a pound box of candy, wrapped in smooth, white paper with gilt lettering, and carried it home, happy as those who come with gifts.

The kitchen was empty. He turned up the gas. A plate, knife, and fork were laid at his place. On the stove was the pot; he lifted the lid and looked inside: roast meat and potatoes. His mother came from the bedroom, a shawl over her night-gown. She looked at him with the large sad eyes he had seen in the museum on the coffins of Alexandrians.

"Sit down, Ma, I want to tell you something."

"Tell me tomorrow." She knew that her son was safe and sound and would be fed that day at least. Now she could fall asleep.

He gave her the box of candy in the plain light of morning. The display of affection was slightly annoying to both. "As soon as you get a little money you must spend it."

She opened the box, and they looked for a moment at the chocolates, each in a frill of colored paper, and breathed their heavy fragrance. Sarah Yetta took one, and he saw how red and rough her hand was, how black its lines. Ezekiel took a chocolate, too, and she covered the box. "This is for the children," and she put it up on the ice-box.

Ezekiel went to the gas company and left a deposit to have the gas turned on. Then he bought the table and chairs. They were delivered that afternoon. He painted them and the soap boxes at night so that they would be dry by morning.

He had to buy popular books outright, but insisted that the others be sent on consignment. He was just beginning, he argued, and had to learn what his trade wanted. Some publishers shipped and some did not.

He began to pay off Mr. Diamond. Some of the books he returned. On the payment of his first month's rent, he secured a lease for a year from the grocer. Until the business was on a firm footing, he took nothing for himself, except what he spent for lunches and a pair of shoes. As Christmas came he did more and more business. His name was lettered on the window, a carpenter put up shelving, he bought another table and two easy-chairs and an oil-stove. Since he had no chairs to begin with, now he had too many.

One Saturday night Ezekiel saw his father staring through the window. Ezekiel beckoned to him, but he would not come in. Ezekiel's sisters, however, came—too often for his liking. When Ezekiel began to pay his mother for his keep, his father became friendly, spoke, sometimes, about the shop in which he worked or his lodge; Ezekiel's sisters were often respectful.

At the bookshop one day was like another. There was much talk, of course, of books and writers. But Ezekiel heard little worthwhile—except when an acquaintance, specializing in French at one of the universities, read him Vildrac's poems, and once, when a stranger who said he was born in Iceland, told him of the sagas.

Ezekiel was free only at night: he became a nocturnal animal. When he thought of the heavens, it was of stars and the moon or of a black sky. The streets for him were dark, except when snow made the pavements and gutter bluish white. Then he did not get home until one or two in the morning. And, sometimes, he would walk one of the bridges to Brooklyn, making a path through the unbroken snow. Nor could the rains of winter that fell steadily as if from a machine keep him indoors.

The ash-carts made their rounds, the empty cans booming as the men set them down in the empty streets. Once Ezekiel came upon a string of camels from a circus walking in the snow, and once, under the elevated railway, there was an elephant in Allen Street. Sometimes he met a man talking to himself. Once a young woman asked him for a nickel; he gave it to her, and she hurried away without a word.

Men and women came into the shop and talked rationally; it was warm beside the oil-stove, the sun shone through the window by day, at night the lamp filled every corner with its soft light. A sane world moved through the street. In the till money accumulated. But the world of his freedom was depopulated, without a sun, of much darkness and silence.

Time and again when Ezekiel talked to the girls that came into his shop, as he pitched word after word upon them, he thought of the sound of coins on sand. Somewhere there must be a woman—so a girl, he thought, dreams of the man she hopes to marry and at last puts up with her husband. (He admitted to himself that a casual chat was hardly one in which to expect a woman with decent reticence to become Eve.) Here and there a woman that passed and was gone, the waves as they curved to become foam and rushing water upon the shore, flowers and trees—the bulky catalogue of the earth's beautiful was still new. He moved through his Eden alone.

One day a young woman came into his shop and picked two books from those on the table. "Send them up this evening," she said.

"If it is not too late, I'll bring them after I close the store. That will be about nine."

"Very well," she said and walked out.

She had on a black coat without braid or trimming, Ezekiel noticed: it was of a rich stuff that glistened slightly as she moved her slim body; the black set off her bright yellow hair. Because the forehead was a little heavy, her eyes had seemed a little sunken. These, too, were large, and against her white skin and yellow hair their deep dull black had been disquietingly beautiful.

He remembered her cold, monotonous voice. He didn't matter: a book-vending machine—that could also promptly deposit the phrases placed in him. He found himself thinking of her hair. He had been sick, but at last on a sunny day he could leave the house, and his eyes were caught by a girl looking into the shop of the florist: her braids had the same light yellow, brighter than any of the flowers in the window, the color the Greeks must have used on the hair of their statues of Apollo. It had begun to rain. Nobody else came into the shop.

It seemed to Ezekiel that his thoughts at last brought out the sun, whose brightness they had been touching and leaving and returning to, as a bird pecks at a golden fruit. The clouds

were disentangled, white and high, as if innocent of the rain.
The routine of the shop began again; his thoughts were gladly
locked away. So Ezekiel, when a child, used to hide a piece of
candy to prolong the expectation of eating it. Without thinking of her, he was cheerful, and knew when he stopped to
think of his cheerfulness, it was because he had seen her and
would see her again that evening.

With the twilight he could no longer keep her out of his
mind. He could see her at the door; she would take the package into her hands; they would be ungloved, the slender wrists
would show, and a little of the forearm in the sleeve. He could
hear her cold, measured "Thank you," and the door would
close. But he would have seen her.

The books she had bought troubled him: an autobiography
and a novel, praised in the book reviews—they were always
discovering masterpieces among the new books. But how
should she know what the books were like until she read at
least a chapter or two? Most likely she would think of them as
he. But he had rather she had asked for *Aucassin and Nicolette*
or the *Saga of Burnt Njal* or *Walden* or—how many others.

At last he was walking up the stoop. "Is Miss Dauthendey
in?" he asked the maid.

"Are those the books? I'll take them," and the door was
closed. He had blown a pretty bubble and it burst in his face.
He enjoyed the joke none the less. She would come again to
buy the books talked of next week or month. And that hope
made the shop fragrant, the prospect of coming back to it
tomorrow and tomorrow and tomorrow not merely the way to
dusty death.

Then he began to weave plots to snare another sight of that
yellow hair and those black eyes, to be as close as he dared to
her. He might come some evening as the owner of a shop with
the interests of his customers at heart and so visiting them

with the new books. Someone had left her glove. He might ask if it were hers—as if he had not watched her gloved hands closely enough.

How silly! But the thoughts of her were not to be shaken easily out of his head; they clung to his brain with many feet and buzzed and pricked.

The lives of insects are brief. Next morning they were dead. Miss Dauthendey had become a memory, tacked up on the wall of his mind, there to fade. Perhaps the candlelight with which he sometimes moved in the attic of old lumber and odds and ends of his life would fall upon Miss Dauthendey for a moment. So, the sight of her, it lit up the girl with yellow hair staring into the florist's shop whom he had seen five—or was it ten years before?

And yet when Miss Dauthendey did come in, as an event comes to justify a dream, he had been expecting her all along. She wore the same black coat, but since the day was warm, she had it unbuttoned. He could see row on row of white lace in a cascade from her throat, and thought of the psalm—"she shall be brought to the king in raiment of needle-work"; his heart kept typing, "My heart is inditing a good matter, my heart is inditing a good matter."

"How did you like"—and he named the two books she had bought. He now saw that her mouth was red without the use of a lipstick, small, and the lips full. They twitched into a momentary smile, but said nothing. Surely the bookseller thought well of them: books, so praised by critics and that sold so well, were to be praised.

If only those ponderous sentences he had forged in his heart would now clothe him in wrought gold, that his wit and imagery would cover him with garments smelling of myrrh and aloes and cassia, that his arrows were sharp in the hearts of his enemies, that his tongue were the pen of a ready writer, as the psalmist boasted. "They are both shoddy books," he began.

She ran her eyes over the titles along the shelves. Perhaps she was listening, and he went on. "Here is a man," he said, "who has read widely, who thinks himself a philosopher and humanitarian. At a slight, the greatness of other people with which the professor has filled himself and thinks his own, leaks away as through a knife-thrust in a water-skin. He is petty as those at whom he is in a rage; he catches their hysteria and becomes hysterical denouncing it. The book is sad, not because of the slights to the writer, unwarranted slights, perhaps, to a Jew, but sad because the man himself is slight. It has the squeaks of a trapped mouse, not the nightingale's song or the sadness of a wave as it bursts into inevitable foam. . . ."

He stopped timidly, not sure of the image he was about to step on or those on which he stood. She glanced at him and smiled: she was listening.

"As for the novel, did you see the note in *The Freeman*?" She shook her head. He had seen the gesture a thousand times. He would never see it again, he thought, without think- ing of her. The yellow hair glistened in two thick braids, coiled neatly upon the back of her head.

"The note was the only thing I ever saw in *The Freeman* worthwhile—but I do not read every issue. Besides, I mean it for praise, because in how few magazines do we see anything worthwhile?" He was becoming tedious. He was sorry he had begun to talk, but he couldn't quit it now. That would be sit- ting down in the puddle. Well, he would sit down. "But I don't suppose you care about the note. Did you like the books?"

"What did it say?" she asked politely. He could not make out whether she was interested or had parried his question.

"The note pointed out that a novel of this type lacks understanding of its characters: it has almost all that they said and did, yet only superficial characteristics—not what is burning at their hearts."

It had begun to rain and now it poured. "You had better stay until it is over. It can't last at this rate." She sat down with a rueful face.

He closed the door, for the rain was beating in, and lit the lamp. Now that she was at the mercy of his speech, Ezekiel was silent. He read the publishers' announcements that had accumulated; Miss Dauthendey settled herself in the chair and picked a book at random from the table. She only managed a sentence or two and turned from the alien words to watch the rain.

Miss Dauthendey had but half listened to Ezekiel. She had long found out that what was said seriously and at length—such as the admonishments of her father—mattered little, and more than seeming to listen was a useless vexation.

In this she was happier than Ezekiel, who seized upon each word. They dissolved in the acid of his mind, and he found so little gold, it was not worth his trouble. And still he read and listened—and complained. Everything went into his mouth to be ground between his teeth, and he ate hugely, like the large mammals that eat grasses of little nourishment.

Many centuries of calm life were in Miss Dauthendey's face, in every motion of her hands and body, in her smooth words. Ezekiel was drawn to her as a ship might find itself in a current that carries it from the tropics to a temperate zone.

Though Miss Dauthendey had not followed Ezekiel, the woman in her took in his fire and the mother his timidity. The men she had known were from the north; she liked his black hair and dark thin face, she relished the acid in his speech.

And Miss Dauthendey was lonely. When she looked at herself in the darkened glass of the window, she could not help thinking how absurd that she should be. And surely next year, next month, perhaps that night, she would meet—and so year after year, until she had been frightened that very morning at a grey hair among the yellow.

So soon! She separated it from the others with trembling fingers. No, she had pulled out a yellow one and there the grey hair shone. She was still in her twenties and growing old. Now a crack, no wider than a hair, showed in the mirror of her serenity, but she knew it would widen and widen until she herself would be engulfed. She was sick of that incurable disease, age, and the first symptom had come.

The rain fell steadily. Ezekiel at his desk thought of Aeneas and Dido caught in the storm. He looked about his cave and smiled: he might pass for Aeneas; though he had not come from Troy, his people did come from a little south of it.

Looking through the papers on his desk became a pretence. "Do you know the work of the German poet with the same name as yours—Max Dauthendey?"

"No, I do not read German," and her eyes fell on her book.

Ezekiel sat calmly in his chair watching the rain. So he seemed to Miss Dauthendey and any passer-by. But he was grovelling on the floor, prancing up and down, beating his head against the walls, and flinging the books about. How exasperating. She was like a princess on one of the glass mountains in fairy-books.

Even these were kissed. But the prince had to wear out seven pairs of iron shoes. He had come to her like a swan singing of books, but she was not Leda, and he was too poor to come in a golden shower. He must come to her like Jove himself, but Jove would sooner perish in his flames than this Semele.

Suppose the rain stopped? She was still reading, but she might put the book down at any moment, look outside, smile and be gone. Before it was too late, he should say, Madam, I know that what I think of you does not matter to anybody but myself. I am the dust beneath your shoes, whom only you can make into Adam—and why should you dirty your hands? But I must speak, as even rocks have speech when they hear you. What I say is not mine, but an echo of your beauty. Forget the speaker in the speech and forgive the speech: it is the echo of yourself. Surely men are blind or dumb, if they keep from crying out as you pass, "You are beautiful!"

Miss Dauthendey, for all the silence, heard what Ezekiel was saying, as she heard him before, sufficiently, though not the words themselves. Perhaps she read it in his glance. So she said, looking up from her book and glancing from the window to Ezekiel, "What weather!"

Ezekiel rejoiced, for she had said, I admit you to my companionship. I may talk to you, sometimes, though to be sure only of the weather; but know that you are no longer a block of wood. With the smoke of my breath I have breathed life into you, and you too may speak of the weather. And Ezekiel did.

"The weather is all right if you are dressed for it. I like to walk in the rain."

And Miss Dauthendey, as if regretting her forwardness, answered, "It isn't raining so heavily now," and with a smile of thanks put the book down and rose.

What an idiot I am, Ezekiel thought, I have hinted that she leave.

And sure enough she turned to the door, buttoned her coat, took hold of the knob, and would have stepped into the rain had not Ezekiel called out, "Please let me lend you this umbrella, if you must go." And he unearthed an umbrella from behind some packages. "Don't hesitate. It isn't mine. Somebody forgot it here a long time ago."

"Are you sure you won't need it yourself?"

"Oh, I'm staying here until nine o'clock. The rain will be

over by then. Please take it." And Ezekiel on the lower step
opened the umbrella and held it over her.

He had been able to do something for one so dear; and in
passing the umbrella to her, had touched her gloved hand. He
was absurdly happy, dressed in scarlet and on his head a wreath
of roses. As if he had eaten a drug, without systole and diastole,
his strength flowed on and cried to the stars for mountains to
sweep away.

To become worthy of her! His eyes fell on an encyclopedia
in thirty volumes he had bought secondhand. Little by little,
until all that knowledge was his! He took down the first volume
and read—about the letter A and its sounds from the guttural
among the Semites to the vowel of the Europeans, of the forty
rivers of Europe named Aa, of Aalborg in Denmark, of Aalen
in Wuertemburg, pleasantly situated on the Kocher, of the Aar
in Switzerland, a beautiful silvery river abounding in fish, of
the aardvark, of Abakansk in Siberia with statues of men, seven
to nine feet high, covered with hieroglyphics no one can read,
of abandonment at law, of Pietro d'Abano, born in Italy about
1250, and Abaris, the Hyperborean, and about abattoirs. He
read on in a missal in which he worshipped his Mary. When
night fell he had reached the history of Abyssinia.

As he closed the shop he remembered he had not eaten that
day. But now in his faintness there was a spice of joy that he
knew would keep him conscious through all the dark streets
and hours. He went over what she had said—as if she had said
anything. With the persistence of a child and its pleasure in a
mechanical toy he made her go through her gestures. English
became a new and rich speech: he modified nouns such as hair,
neck, throat, mouth, gloves, eyes, body by *her*, and *she* was the
subject and *her* the object of verbs.

* * *

Miss Dauthendey came into the shop just before closing time, later in the week, to return the umbrella. She thanked him, lingered over the table of new books, and was about to go, when both were startled at the sound of rain (though it had been cloudy all day). She looked at Ezekiel and burst out laughing.

Ezekiel was going to give her the umbrella, but he said, "I'm closing in five minutes; if the rain isn't over by that time, may I see you home?" She nodded.

The rain was not over by that time: it looked as if it would rain all night and the next day, too.

"But you are getting wet," she said as they walked along. "Come under the umbrella." Their arms touched; he was glad the night hid his face.

"You are a stranger in the city, aren't you?" he asked.

"Yes."

"I can tell you're no New Yorker by your *r*s." Ezekiel added, "I suppose you've seen the sights."

"I haven't walked across the Brooklyn Bridge."

Inexpert as he was, this was too obvious not to grasp. "May I take you there next Sunday?"

"If you wish."

Miss Dauthendey, alone in her room on the fourth floor, pulled off her shoes and stockings: her feet were wet. She let her braids down—she might as well go to bed—and her clothes tumbled on a chair, she snapped the light off.

She thought of the town she had left: the lawns and gardens, the shade trees lifting the pavement blocks, the street crowded —with leaves and twigs. Her large black eyes were closed, and ordinary tears flowed between the lids to the cotton pillowcase.

Was it so tedious? How foolish she was. How good they all were and how ungrateful she had been; how kind their letters;

how cruel to leave her father alone. Suppose he were sick? How selfish of her.

Miss Dauthendey pulled the blanket over her head. She wept for her sins, until her eyes were dry and only the lashes wet. Then she straightened her knees and came from under the blanket. The air of the room was fresh. Her bed was mussed, and she smoothed it in the dark. She put her hand on the pillow and for a moment was surprised to find it damp.

When she woke the sunlight was streaming between the blind and sill into the darkness of the room. As she dressed Miss Dauthendey began to sing. She sang softly, not to disturb her neighbors. But the sparrows outside were not so polite. They sang, too, and their loudest.

On Sunday Ezekiel was waiting in the hail. At a step on the stairs he looked up, and Miss Dauthendey was smiling down to him. He hardly knew how he found himself beside her in the sunny, silent street.

Towards evening they had tea and macaroons in a pastry shop. A fire was blazing on the hearth—a stingy fire. Ezekiel and Miss Dauthendey, however, found it cheerful. They watched the ugly slats of the grocer's boxes turning into flame and the indolent walk of the waitress, a mulatto, graceful as a panther.

Ezekiel became interested in some large cakes. "What are those?" he asked the waitress.

"Brioches."

"Have they cream inside?"

"No."

They were served two each; Ezekiel ate his—a sort of sponge cake, but Miss Dauthendey just tasted hers. "Filling, isn't it?" he said. She smiled.

That he who in the routine of the shop could say fine things, would become on a Sunday, as Dante says of Virgil, a river of speech—and he had been dumb for blocks. And when he did speak! "There's the Woolworth Building, the Metropolitan" (he knew all along she had seen them the first week, if not her first day in town). "It's nice to walk on this wooden planking. What lovely twilights we have in New York. Filling, isn't it?"

But on Wednesday night she came into the shop. Ezekiel was talking to a customer; another was poking among the books. Speech dried up in Ezekiel's mouth and after a word or two, the customer left. Ezekiel went up to Miss Dauthendey, smiled, and could not say a word.

She asked for a book, the favorite that week, and as he wrapped it, opened her purse.

"Oh, no, please show no money."

"Oh, but really—."

"Really, I can't take money"—from you, he was about to say—"from friends. Please," and he put the book in her hand. He thought, Had I diamonds and pearls...

From Heine he jumped to Ben Jonson's

> Indian shells,
> Dishes of agate, set in gold, and studded
> With emeralds—.

"If I had a golden pound to spend," Francis Ledwidge sang. And Ezekiel, with all this prompting, could say nothing.

"Then I can never come in for a book again."

"But why buy books of that sort? They are not worth keeping: tasting, yes—remember your Bacon. Come and borrow them, but don't spend good money on them."

"Do you tell that to everybody?"

"We do lend books, you know, to everybody." The door closed. The other customer had gone. "It's time to lock up."

When they were on the sidewalk, "May I see you home?" he asked.

"It's too nice to go home," and she looked up at the stars. The night was warm, too, for the season. "I'd like to get away from streets and houses."

"The park?"

She did not answer, but walked towards Fifth Avenue. The bus was crowded, and there were no seats to be had together. At Fifty-ninth Street, where Central Park's reservoir of trees, bushes and grass begins, he looked at her. Would she stay on just for a bus ride? But after ten blocks or so, she rose. On the sidewalk, she leaned against him for a moment, as if still swaying on the lurching bus. He took her arm to steady her, and she did not draw away.

They entered the park upon a winding path and left the glare along Fifth Avenue to face the serried lights of the apartment houses on the other side. "It is impossible to get away," Ezekiel said.

The path turned through a thicket of trees to a lawn. "Let us sit here," and Miss Dauthendey walked boldly on the grass. Ezekiel followed, but looked about for a policeman. She sat down in the gloom of the trees and took off her hat.

Not a house was to be seen. Only the asphalt walk had followed them from the sidewalks of the city and now lay waiting in a curve. Ezekiel wondered whether the light was from the moon or an electric lamp. The thicket behind them rose almost in a wall. A single tree was on the lawn, not a leaf to hide its grace.

Miss Dauthendey stirred beside him. "Are you comfortable?" he asked.

She had stretched out and was resting on her left elbow, plucking at the withered grass with her right hand. Her coat, which she had buttoned, her black shoes and stockings were lost in the darkness; her face was only a blur. "Yes," she answered, but turned to lie on her back, her hands folded under her head.

They were on a knoll, and her feet sloped downward. She seemed comfortable enough to Ezekiel, and he turned to watch the tree on the lawn. The branches rippled from the trunk like rays from the head of Epstein's Sun God.

Miss Dauthendey whispered. He leaned across to hear. His hand slid over the withered grass, pebbles, and the castings of earthworms, until it stopped at her coat. "What?" he asked. She did not answer. He lowered his head. Still she did not stir—she pulled her head away, "No, no," she said and sat up.

He moved close to her and caught her in his arms. He kissed her cheek, his lips found hers and pressed until her mouth opened, and her teeth clicked against his. She pushed his face away. He lifted his head, but still held her in his arms. She snuggled to him. I suppose I ought to kiss her again, he thought.

He would rather watch in quiet the tree on the lawn whose branches rippled out in a fan. It was clear to him that he did not care for Miss Dauthendey. But here she was, a breathing woman in his arms, a load he had caught up; and must now carry some distance before he could put it down. His cue as Romeo had sounded, and he shuffled out upon the stage. He began to kiss Miss Dauthendey, but it was too mechanical. "Let's go, I'm chilly," and she shivered.

She crossed the dimly lit lawn to the asphalt path. Ezekiel turned to see, and sure enough it was an electric light, not the moon. He took her arm, but Miss Dauthendey moved away from him, and they walked along in silence.

Inside the bus, Miss Dauthendey took a little mirror out of her purse and keeping her eyes from Ezekiel, fixed her hair. Ezekiel saw her face sharp as a collie's and the dull rouge on her cheeks. He looked at her yellow hair with suspicion. "What a sight I am," she said at last and glanced at Ezekiel, smiling as she dropped her eyes.

He smiled back. "A heavenly sight," he whispered. It was crude, but she liked it. When he helped her from the bus, she leaned heavily against him.

She whispered, "How rough your chin is, my face is all sore. I'll have to put cold cream on it." Just before turning into the street where she lived, she said, "Let's say good-by here," and lifted her lips. Dutifully he lowered his head and kissed her. Then he unbuttoned her coat and thrusting his arm about her waist, pressed her to him and kissed her until she turned her head.

"Let's have lunch together tomorrow," he said.

"That's too soon."

"Then tomorrow night?" She nodded.

"Shall I call for you?"

"No, I'll drop into the store."

He supposed it his duty to stand on the corner and watch until she entered the house.

All of next day Ezekiel had been thinking of her and had left to his fingers the work of the bookshop. In the evening, as he waited, his heart was uneasy: he understood the valentines. When she came at last, they smiled to each other, and neither said a word. What a relief, Ezekiel thought, to be rid of the clumsy medium of speech.

The store was empty: he could put out the light at once. She stood in the doorway; he brushed against her and the next minute held her in his arms. She leaned back and he kissed her twice on the lips, long snug kisses in the dark.

She rested her head against his breast. Ezekiel kissed the

nape of her neck, pressing his left cheek against her hair and his right against the collar of her coat.

She kept her head lowered, and he had to kiss on until she stirred in his arms and moved away.

How quiet the world had become. Usually, when he locked the shop and escaped into the street, longings—to paint, to hear music, to study all the sciences, to keep on with his reading of the encyclopedia (he had made little headway since the first day), to walk around the earth—pecked and pecked at him, swirled about and dropped their dung upon him; but now he was alone with a woman—he smiled at the thought of Miss Dauthendey as a scarecrow—and the sky was empty. Thankful for this peace, he stopped suddenly as they were walking along and putting his arm about her, drew her to him. She yielded at once and lifted her face for him to kiss.

"Where shall we eat?" he asked, after a while. "You must be starved, it's so late."

"I'm not hungry at all."

"I don't know where to go at this hour." Far down the street were the white lights of a restaurant. "Child's?" and he smiled apologetically. She walked towards it.

"Do you know, I don't know your name."

"Jane."

A good, plain, but odd name, he thought, for a girl with blond hair and black eyes—and who walked as if she were about to fly.

"What are you thinking of?"

"That you walk as if you were about to fly: a German wrote that—Rainer Maria Rilke."

"My grandfather was German."

"And your grandmother Spanish?"

"No, she was a Jewess."

His arms trembled and he wanted to press her to himself

again, but the lights of the restaurant were too near. He had to be content with squeezing her hand and dropping a kiss on it.

How sure he had been that she would not be friendly, because he was a Jew. And then, when she had let him kiss her, had rested in his arms, he thought, Perhaps she does not know what I am, perhaps in the town she comes from there are only two or three Jews, and she does not know them as surely as those do who live in cities. Yes, it is sometimes hard to tell Jews from Latins. When he told the story of Heine and a girl in Paris to a Jew who had lived in St. Louis, that had happened to him, too. In the friendliest of talks, the girl, despite his name and face, which he thought Jewish enough, told him how she loathed Jews. He revenged himself telling her what he was—all a joke to Heine and the Jew from St. Louis, but it had come out of limbo to trouble Ezekiel.

And even if she did not dislike Jews, were there not irreconcilables between them? If his grandfather crawled under the stove during a pogrom, his grandmother saw in it the wisdom of the reed. But now there was the bond of blood between Jane Dauthendey and himself: she could despise him, but not for being a Jew. He was not Sisera: the stars in their courses were not fighting against him. And he knew himself drawn to her because of the Jewess, that renegade her grandmother, because of the dark eyes that looked from the trappings of her blond beauty.

"I don't think I ever told you much about my folks," he said. "My father is what is known as an operator: he sews caps. He used to work at wrappers, and even became a foreman. But wrappers went out of style, no woman would wear them. He tried this and that, lost what little he had saved, and was glad to make a living again at his sewing machine. My father is not an old man: he is in his forties. But the kind of work he has been doing has made an old man of him—stooping over a sewing machine for twenty years. When I was a kid, he once took me to the shop, just to show off with me, I guess. I must have been on my vacation from school, because I remember it was in the summer, and the day was hot. The sewing machines stood against a blank wall under a row of gas-lamps. There were only two windows, and these were in the far end of the shop. My father led me to one of the machines and put his hand upon it affectionately. 'This is mine,' he said proudly. And why not? Work meant pay, and what were we more afraid of than slack? Then Ma had to ask the grocer and the butcher to trust her and we kids, my sisters and I, got no more pennies. Pa would hang around the house in broad day and was cranky, and my sisters and I couldn't play the way we used to."

They had walked into the white light of many lamps that shone again from the white ceiling, the white marble tops of the tables, the white tile floor, the white china, nickel fittings and cutlery, glasses of water, white suits of the waiters. As she sat opposite, how beautiful Jane was. Ezekiel wondered that he had ever thought otherwise.

When she poured the cream over her baked apple, he smiled at the harmonious note added to the glistening whites about them. And what contrast in the black coffee, and in the dark brown to which the cream changed it.

"What are you smiling at?" she asked.

"At the brown of this toast and this yellow pat of butter."

"You look like an advertisement for some bread."

"When the sun shines everything has color; then we see the sky blue, the grass green, and so forth—you know all that. Now, I have gone into restaurants, this restaurant, often enough; can you guess why it is that only now the yellow of the butter, the brown of the toast—why Child's has become so beautiful that if I could paint, I would rush away to put it on canvas after canvas? Can you guess the sun that has brought out these colors?"

She smiled into his face and tapped his foot with hers. His breath came thick and fast, his hands and knees trembled, he bit his lower lip to steady himself. "I ought to lay hands on you for that," he whispered. Would it be too mad to lean across the table and catch her head in his hands, feel again the curves of her face and her yellow hair in his fingers?

"Why do you look away?"

"To keep the sun out of my eyes."

When they were in the night again, "Where shall we go?" he asked. "To the park?"

"It's too late to go anywhere, and I'm tired."

They reached the stoop of her house; he stopped and was about to say good-by. "Come up," she said.

He followed with a beating heart. She unlocked the hall door and he walked in like a thief, stepping softly on the carpet. He studied its threadbare spots. She climbed the stairs slowly, tired and sad. They met nobody, and he was glad for her sake, though she did not seem to care.

When they reached the last flight she stopped to rest and turned to look at Ezekiel. He took her arm. "Are you tired?" he asked. And for the rest of the way she leaned against him.

At her door she opened her purse and took out the key. The dim light of the hail shone on the long shank. She fitted the key into the lock, turned it, and they entered. Ezekiel felt that they had performed a rite together.

She lit the electric lamp on the dresser, went to the closet and hung up her hat and coat. "Throw your coat there," she said, pointing to the couch. He obeyed and sat down in the cane armchair. "Will you smoke?" and she took a cigarette from the package on the table. He shook his head.

The smoke of her cigarette drifted before the miniature sun above the dresser. Ezekiel remembered a Japanese picture of mist on the hills, and anger at war blazed up in him.

"What are you angry at? You made the funniest face."

"I was just thinking about war with Japan."

She broke into a little laugh. "What on earth makes you think of that now? You're a queer bird."

They sat on in the silence, grateful for the peace they had unlocked. Ezekiel imagined himself prehistoric man with his mate in a snug cave. He looked with friendly eyes at the door which shut them in together. Through the window behind him he could see a light here and there, but the houses across the street were dark.

"Does the light hurt your eyes?" she asked. "I'll turn it off." He wondered at her boldness. She stood up and snapped the light off, but crossing the room, lit the lamp on the table. "That's better, isn't it?"

She pressed the burning end of her cigarette on the ashtray and took her seat again. He studied the bit of cigarette sticking up. His lips were dry, and now and then he moistened them as if to speak, but could say nothing. "Are you comfortable there?" she said at last. "Sit back, don't sit on the edge of the chair."

He waited a little before answering. "I'm not comfortable at all," he said and got to his feet. He sat down on the couch beside her and pressed his mouth against hers until her lips parted and her breath was warm on his face. She lay limp and heavy in his arms. As his fingers ran through her hair, he felt the hairpins. "I'm hurting you," he said and began to take them out.

She pushed him away and standing free of him, loosened her hair. He placed the hairpins he held upon the dresser and bent to pick up those she had let fall. "Oh, never mind," she said. "How rough your face is," and she stroked his chin. "You did not think of me this morning, else you would have shaved."

"But I did shave."

She had put her arms about his neck and was lifting her face to his. "You do like me a little, don't you?" she murmured.

He kissed her lightly, and trembling, began to unbutton the collar of her waist. "No, no," she said and placed her fingers upon his, but there was no strength in her hand.

He bared the long, white throat. As he kissed it, her arms tightened about him. Her head hung back, the eyes shut, the mouth slightly open. He could see a shoulder strap of her underwear, the flesh beneath it white and smooth, and he slipped his hand under the bit of ribbon.

He drew his hand out. At that moment the wave withdrew and left all his walls and towers. He was like a jumper who has taken a running start and stops himself just before the leap: beyond was anarchy. "Jane," he said, "Jane darling, I am going."

She opened her eyes. "Going?" she said. "So soon?" Her eyes grew moist. She caught hold of his fingers and twisted them. He wrenched them free and reached for his overcoat. She put her hand on his arm. "Where are you going?" she asked.

"Home."

"You are not going to leave me alone, are you?"

"I am." He was surprised at his calmness.

"How cruel you are," she murmured.

"If I stayed, I should be. Suppose I stayed and came again, once or twice, and then never came again, would that not be more cruel?"

"What do you mean? You love me, don't you?"

"I think you are the most beautiful woman I ever saw—at least that I can remember." Her lips twisted in a smile at the qualification. She buttoned the collar of her waist. He could see a tear in the sleeve at the armpit and wondered if he had made it. "But I don't think that I love you," he went on, "that is, want you enough now to think that I'd want you always. If I did, I'd stay."

"You talk too much. Who wants you to stay? Get out!" He stared at her mouth to make sure the harsh voice was hers.

She was standing behind the chair, gripping its back. The light from the table fell across the white of her knuckles.

He put on his overcoat slowly. "Good-night," he said, his right hand on the door-knob. She was out from behind the chair and across the room and had thrown her arms about him.

"Oh, don't go, don't leave me here all alone. You do love me, you know you do. If you didn't, you would—and then throw me aside. But you do love me. Why are you so cruel?"

He stroked the hair from her face and kissed her forehead. "But Jane darling," he began.

"Don't call me darling, you don't mean it."

He was a god who leaned from Heaven pitying himself and her, in the net they themselves wove as the generations before them. "Jane, please listen: I want to get out of my shop and I don't know what I'm going to do—or can do. Why should I drag you into the mess? Stop to think."

"Oh, thinking will never get you anywhere; just follow your instincts and you'll come out all right. Why should you worry about my affairs? That's none of your business." They were silent for a moment, Ezekiel in meditation on what she had said.

"I have no right to let you be foolish. And if I stay, we both shall be," he added smiling. I should have thought of all that, he reproached himself, before I kissed her. He went on aloud, "Come now, go to bed like a good little girl. You are tired and overstrained."

He tried to carry her to the couch, but she was too heavy for him. He could barely lift her from the floor and staggered. She laughed and freed herself from his arms. "When shall I see you again?" she asked calmly.

"Tomorrow," he said politely, but hoped not: he had had enough dramatics for a while.

Jane heard it in his voice. "No," she said. "Go on now, you were in such a hurry to go; what are you standing there for?"

"Good-night," he said and was about to go.

"Aren't you going to kiss me good-night?"

He went through the performance in fine style, he thought, though kissing had become as disgusting to him as to a China-man, and he closed the door gently behind him. Thank God! he thought. When he was safe on the floor below, he stopped to wipe his forehead with his handkerchief.

Well, a situation he had often hoped to be in—and behold, Jokanaan! There should have been asterisks across that part of the story and instead, almost a sermon, the Sermon on the Mount—Venusberg. But he, Ezekiel, was no worshipper of Jeho-vah of the Essenes or Diana: rather like Joseph, no ascetic, but a man who could say on an occasion, "How can I do this great wickedness?" And he amused himself with the thought of Joseph running about the corridors of the palace in his under-wear, his outer garment in the hands of Potiphar's wife.

What a lie, the mess he was in: he didn't care enough about her. It was his conceit that made him think she wanted more than an adventure, *him* always. If he had stayed, would not this the body had been whispering become loud again and again and he bondman to a habit? That was the Jew: you with your Torah, your prohibitions. No, that was Christian: the Jews merely circumcised their desires. And all his bearded ancestors, Ezekiel thought, applauded.

Next day Ezekiel wanted to see her, but he had made up his mind against it. The thought that it would be unfair to her held him to his resolution—and the hope that she would come into the store. But she did not all that week.

Sunday he set himself to walk away from her and kept it up, over Brooklyn Bridge, through Prospect Park, down Ocean Parkway, past Washington Cemetery and the old racing track, trying to tread down the longing to ring her doorbell. He reached Brighton Beach and walked the length of Coney

Island, crunching the shells. The little waves tumbled in out of the blue water and the sky was clear.

The twilight had begun. How often had he seen the coming of the stars and still it moved him, as a cadence in stanza after stanza. So, he thought, men become used to the round of the seasons and of sunshine, twilight, night, and dawn, and the old hate to die. But the young are still indifferent and go to war and upon hazardous ventures. In the train he sat tired, chilled, and unhappy; back in Delancey Street, he could not bring himself to go home.

What a smell! A pimpled waiter was wiping the table. "What'll it be today?" he asked cheerfully. "Potato soup, borsht, potatoes in sour cream..."

Should he order foods he had never tasted in the hope of the exquisite? He realized that the policy of his life was in his choice. Certainly, the old was better: he would be sure of some satisfaction. So he ordered toast and tea and a baked apple. He suspected, too, that the Romans were fonder of eggs and apples than of their pickled carps' tongues or pearls dissolved in vinegar. He ate slowly, to taste each morsel to the utmost, and praised God.

The waiter had fished a dab of butter from the jar behind the counter, written a secret on a little pad, and hidden the slip under the edge of the sugar bowl. Ezekiel, as he ate, studied the delicate curves of the thumbprint on the butter. What a pity to spoil it, he thought, and had none of it.

Afterwards, in a theater near by, clowns were hopping about the stage, riding bicycles, falling off, sliding down chutes, and turning somersaults to the enthusiasm of the musicians. Ezekiel went away.

In a side street, where the stores were few and dimly lit, he could see the stars. They comforted him as they had comforted his ancestors in Chaldea. He began to consider the prodigality of nature, how each plant has plenty of seeds, almost all, if not all, to be lost, and wondered if this were so of the stars, if of all only a few were to be more than seeds. He thought of the Greek myth of the god who ate his children. That any of the stars should live on pleased him, though how unlikely that the earth would be among them—or a planet of this system. The ancient darkness would outlast the greater light and the lesser light; the epilogue would be spoken in the freezing night. And Ezekiel's heart beat rapidly at the thought of how comforting it would be to hold Jane in his arms again, feel her body against his, and see her blond hair close to his eyes. He smiled to think that, examining the machinery of nature, he was caught in it.

There was no light in her window: she was out or asleep. He would see her tomorrow, early in the morning. Whatever resistance she could make was brittle, any wall she might hide behind was eggshell. But in the soberness of the morning he went to his shop and soon the business of the day crowded her into a corner.

Just before closing time she came in and kept her face to the books. When the last customer was gone, she went up to Ezekiel and looking him in the eyes, placed her hand upon his breast and said, "Why are you angry at me?" He caught her in his arms and kissed her.

She freed herself. "Suppose someone should come in?" He wondered what had made her careful. "Your shop would get a nice reputation," she added. "But you didn't come to see me all this while," and she placed her hand upon his breast again and looked into his eyes.

"No," he answered stupidly.

"How nice and curly your hair is," and she stroked it from his forehead.

He pushed her away gently. "My lips can't talk when you do that."

"But who wants them to?"

She played with a button of his shirt. Her hand was heating his blood. "You did not know that I had come; but I was there, my body left to blunder on wherever it was. Last night I took it along and we stood in front of your house, but your window was dark. Were you asleep or out?"

"I was lying on my bed, awake in the loneliness of the night." She turned away. "Oh, why are you torturing yourself so and me?" she said, as if to herself. Then she looked him full in the face. "Whatever can happen to me can only be what nature intended and I am not afraid. Why should you be?"

Ezekiel became cold and hard. "You have not understood me. I understand you, that is easy enough, but you do not understand me. That is why I will have nothing to do with you, because although between my body and yours there are ties, as between my body and perhaps any woman's, between my mind and yours there are none." He groped for words with which to stone her in revenge for his longing. Jane Dauthendey was rigid, not a finger moved. She felt her lips pressed together, her head pushed forward. She stared at Ezekiel until her eyes began to smart, yet she could not lower the lids.

She turned and walked as quickly as she could to her room, and sat on the bed in the darkness, her bosom heaving. After a while she took off her hat and put it on the chair and tried to hang her coat over the back. It slid to the floor. She turned to the bed and flung herself face down; she imagined the pillow her mother and hugged it. How stupid it all was. She was afraid her sobs would be heard—the partitions were thin, she could hear her neighbors; and she buried her face in the pillow.

The doorbell rang. It was he. She sat up. She couldn't let him see her now. Oh, she would never see him again. Her hands went mechanically to her hair. The doorbell rang again.

She heard the steps of the maid along the hall. Then the steps began to climb, one flight and another. Now they stopped at her door. It was he! There was a knock and the maid said, "Miss Dauthendey?"

Should she answer? "Yes?" she said.

"There's a gentleman to see you, Ma'am."

"Oh, I can't see anybody now."

"I'll tell him so, Ma'am. Good-night."

"Good-night."

She laughed softly and lit the light. She combed and brushed her hair. There was no hurry: if he cared he would wait. Her eyes were red, but that would not matter in the dark.

She walked softly downstairs and out upon the stoop. How warm the night was: March the lamb. Ezekiel hurried to her. She put her hand over his mouth and they walked up the street. He held her arm tightly. "Are you trying to break it off?" she asked.

Ezekiel was annoyed at her banter: how lightly she took what he had said. "It was stupid of me to say what I did."

"Of course."

"I had to tell you this tonight: I care too much for you to let you cheapen yourself. I should like to serve seven years for you, as Jacob did; I should like to wear out seven pairs of iron shoes as princes do in fairy books, before I reach you. I am going to place you on a glass mountain and climb to you." He saw her head bent towards him, and she was smiling. Of course, he cared: wasn't she beautiful? "What am I, anyway? I care too much for you to see you waste yourself upon me."

"You're a liar," she said calmly.

"I am," he answered cheerfully, as if this were only another instance of his inferiority to other men.

Jane was lifting her mouth again to his. He kissed it. What

a fool he would be to push her away. What was better in his fingers than this warm, smooth flesh? All the singing of birds was only echoes or faint anticipations of her voice. A great wave rose out of the sea and blotted out the walls and towers he had so laboriously built, drowned all his captains and chosen men: horses and riders were thrown into the sea. What did anything else matter? She was the earth and he, the flaming sun.

Ezekiel had a faint recollection of some resolution he had taken a long time before, as long ago as an hour; but the poor thing now lay drowned, huddled on the shore, unimportant as a jellyfish.

"Ma," his father shouted, "I'm going to the barber." Ezekiel had often asked his father not to shout (though he himself would shout, too). To this his father would say, "In my house I am boss," or "Parents bring up children, not children parents," or— if playful—"Why have you this?" and pinching the lobes would try to stuff them into Ezekiel's ears. Or else he would cry out, "In the shop I have the foreman and the boss, here I have him." When he was energetic, he would answer Ezekiel with a blow.

His visits to the barber-shop annoyed Ezekiel, too. On a Sunday morning his father would spend two or three hours waiting for his "next." "Why do you waste so much of your one free day? Why don't you use a safety-razor?" Ezekiel would say. "And it's cleaner and cheaper."

"It's enough for me that I have lived to see a son use a safety-razor," Saul would answer.

Sarah Yetta always took her husband's part; perhaps, because she felt that he was the weaker; perhaps, because in that ideal family towards which she tried to shepherd hers, the father was the all-wise head, respected and obeyed. And Ezekiel's father felt it natural to talk loud: the machines shouted, God thunders, lions roar, the waves crash, the winds howl, all the strong speak in a loud voice, and—thank God!—he was still of them.

As for the barber-shop, he was not so accustomed to dissect his feelings as to be able to explain why he liked that very wait which his son thought a waste of time. Really, when his "next" came, he was sorry. There were, to begin with, the other customers, neighbors and friends; they talked over the news, how work was coming on in their shops, news of the union, news of the world, all spiced with witticisms. There he would sit in the comfortable cane-bottom chair and rest. During a lull in the talk he would read a newspaper. All the newspapers were there, he did not have to buy any. This little saving was pleasant. The barbers, too, were always polite: he was a customer; and that made him feel important. And the shop had such a good smell: bay rum and the violet perfume of talcum powder. Now and then a customer ordered a hair tonic. This sent a sharp pleasant odor into the air. And then the luxury of stretching out and, utterly passive, to feel the blade take a week's growth of beard from his face. How could he explain all this to his son who in a contemptuous voice was urging him to use a safety-razor?

That afternoon Ezekiel entered the Oriental rooms of the Metropolitan Museum and found himself before a Buddha. Here there were hardly any visitors though it was Sunday. In the silence he gazed at the placid face until his own turbulence became a lotus pool.

To see a painting or a statue, he thought, and then to look out of the window, is to see how fresh and richer life itself is. He had read this a few weeks before in the volume of a German philosopher, and because Ezekiel had always felt so, the sentence had significance. To others it might be only platitudinous.

He would not think at all now: it was Sunday. He gave himself up to his eyes. The images of the world glided over him and as upon a pool did not leave a ripple.

Saul Rubinov clinked the stone of the last of his prunes on the meat plate. "Ma, let's go somewhere tonight."

The children smiled to see their mother's excitement. Sarah Yetta had her coat on and was looking for her hat. "What do you want a hat for?" asked Mr. Rubinov impatiently. He was wondering whether it would not have been wiser for him to have gone to bed.

She was almost at the door when she burst out laughing. "Look at this!" and she held her coat open. "I nearly went with my apron on."

"Where are we going?" she asked. Mr. Rubinov to tease her said nothing. They came at last to a motion-picture house. Bright lights lit up its huge posters. The air inside was foul, but they were used to it in no time.

At midnight, their eyes dazed by the flicker of the pictures on the screen, they found the lights before the posters out and only a few pushcarts still in the street. "Twenty cents thrown away," said Mr. Rubinov. "Such foolishness!"

"It was not thrown out. We need a little pleasure, too. We should go once in a while like other people to the movies, to a friend's house: that's the way people live."

"I have nothing better to do. Look at her, always ready to run around, the mother of five children and still a—." Mr. Rubinov went through his meagre vocabularies of Russian, Hebrew, and English for a suitable word to crush her, and left the sentence unfinished.

He stopped at a stand where slices of coconut were float-
ing in a dish of water. "Well, Mamma," he said and pointed,
"I know you like it."

Sarah Yetta turned her eyes away. "No, Saul, so late at
night." Her husband did not press the matter, but bought himself a package of his brand of cigarettes.

"Another cent," he said sternly to the stand-keeper, who had
given him his change. The man slowly put another cent on the
oilcloth-covered board. "On Delancey Street for two packages
it is still half a cent cheaper," added Mr. Rubinov.

"Make a living these days," said the stand-keeper bitterly to
the night. But Mr. Rubinov having won his cent walked on
serenely.

When he was little, he had a book from the library in which the
frontispiece showed Roland ambushed in the mountain pass:
his back to a rock, his head lifted, blowing his horn. Whenever
he found himself troubled, Ezekiel liked to think himself
Roland. Now he also thought of himself as a tree, sending its
roots far and wide through the black earth, pushing stones
aside or encircling them: "he shall be like a tree planted beside
the streams of water." He had read the Psalms too late, though,
to think of himself first as such; and, perhaps, it is more natural for a man to think himself a warrior than a tree....

What had he done? So, he imagined, a king declares war and
enters upon excited and unhappy years. It was too late: the
proclamation had been made, the trumpets sounded throughout the land. In the buildings Ezekiel passed on the way to his
shop were only factories; along the streets waited or clattered
express wagons; on the walks were errand boys, and men, their
faces set, their feet on errands. What an unhappy world, now
his.

He looked at those beside him. He ought not to do this: a man in business to sit on a park bench in broad day with men out of work and nursemaids. He had enlisted in an army doomed to defeat in spite of all its victories, and must serve his term.

Even in an hour it would begin again. He must buy this book and that to sell to this man and this man, to this woman and this woman, every one who might buy. So Alexander must have felt when he had conquered an empire to find another— no end to his task. It was the warfare of the sun, its rays too short for space, too brief for time, against night.

He heard the high-pitched conversation of the sparrows. He was glad that he was not Solomon: it is enough to have to overhear the speech of man, he thought. If he understood the chatter of birds too, the buzz of flies, how could he ever listen to himself? Then, as with a faucet, he turned off the thoughts splashing into the sink of his mind. He sat, a stone image, his feet on asphalt, overhead the long grey clouds, and looked quietly at the sombre world. Men came and went. Still he sat there, his stone heart calm, his stone mind untroubled by thoughts, his stone fingers in his lap, his feet without walking to do. The noisy city rushed about him, a brook about a stone.

New Year's Day Ezekiel went through his stock. He had money in the bank; he had made a living and had trade and credit.

He was cold. There was only enough heat to keep the water pipes from freezing. Outside the wind was howling. The yellow wires of the electric lamp shone in its glass bulb.

He turned the light off; with numbed fingers he locked the door. The narrow street was silent, except for his own steps. Down and down the street he went, past the closed doors—a Pharaoh who had escaped from his pyramid. Through the streets, corridors of stone, he walked, disembowelled, thin and stiffly erect in the wind.

The next day the work of the new year would begin. He was already twenty-two. This business—in this very air in which he had begun to breathe, he found himself choking. The shop had taken root: he had brought fire to man; but he himself was tied down, Prometheus on the Caucasian rock.

In a restaurant he warmed his hands on a cup of coffee and sipped it slowly, without sugar, without cream, a black, bitter drink. It warmed and strengthened him. It seemed to him that the bitter night of his life—he would drink it so, mouthful by mouthful, and stand up, warm and strong.

If he had studied music, if he could draw and paint... Some of those he had known at school were socialists. What good trying to change material conditions, if men are still the same? But how can men better their spiritual conditions, if they need their time and energy for bread? they would argue. To each his work, he would think; my work is with the spirit of man. He would never say this; they were too clever to let him escape in an ambiguity, like a god in a cloud.

The stars burned brightly; the glow of the street lights could not hide them. Time and again they had comforted him in their array, or sometimes—just one, like a messenger those who lived in the days of the judges sometimes met. As each atom was like the solar system, so he, too, and all about him, going their ways, were led securely as the stars.

He came to City Hall Park. The morning newspapers were out. In the morning he would have to join the rest in the hunt for business, more business, never enough: the maw of the shop would stretch to hold all he could get. Book and book of last year were played out, dead as last year; new books, but the same business, the old futility.

* * *

He would divide his life. So God divided the world into earth and sky. So He divided the earth into land and water. The shop was land; on this he could build walls and houses, plant vineyards and fig trees, but his other life would be like the ocean, without a master—except, perhaps, the moon.

Ezekiel reached Central Park West and there was the moon, like a good omen, above the trees. These too were his allies: they had helped him often enough. The trees stood at attention as he passed, but the lines of these veterans were broken; sometimes they were grouped on a hill, sometimes scattered on a lawn. As he walked down One-hundred-and-tenth Street to Fifth Avenue, he saw the glimmer of the street-lamps on the lake. It lay among all the asphalt and brick, alive, fed by deep springs. His other life would be like that, he thought, neither syrup nor bitters. He was Janus; towards the world he would turn one face, but the other must be turned away. So, he thought, his grandfather Ezekiel went about the country on business, writing page after page of verse to hide in his baggage—until his widow found the bulky manuscript and burnt it.

"Will you come home late again?" Sarah Yetta asked in a voice from which she tried to smooth all anxiety.

Ezekiel looked at her, hesitated, and said: "Maybe; I think so," and went out.

She would have liked to ask him where he was going—what he was doing. He used to tell her himself, and now that he did not, he was hiding something. And if she asked he would lie, perhaps, or be silent—go farther and farther from her. She sighed.

It seemed to her that if she only had had time to read when she was young, she would have patterned her life on the wisdom in the books and lived wisely and happily. So, time and again, she had spread a pattern carefully on cloth and cut others a garment that fit and was becoming. And yet her son with all the education so cheap in America, this blessed land—Sarah Yetta took up her long fork to turn the meat in the pot. As she lifted the cover the steam rose and gathered in a mist on her eyeglasses.

Ezekiel walked slowly along the street. He was not to be at Jane's room for some time. It had become somewhat tiresome —the sweet false words, the flavorless true ones. But they were unimportant, of course. He stopped to look at a store window. The store had been a restaurant, but now had been empty for months. In the window there was still a dusty sign—"All Kinds of Soft Drinks for Sale"; bottles of "near beer" and soda had been grouped in a pattern about a rubber plant. This had been taken away, and all that was left was a leaf, tightly curled, in two shades of brown, the darker spreading from the middle like a stain. Most of the bottles, still tightly capped, had burst; the liquid had run out and dried on the dusty oil-cloth. Some of it had soaked into the gauze curtain in back that shut off the window from the store, and there were faint uneven marks along the dusty cloth where it had been wet. The beer bottles had burst into many pieces—even the thick bottoms were cracked and broken—but two bottles of orange-colored soda were still in their places, whole and alive in the sunshine. The others were out of place, and whatever the design might have been, it was no more. A bit of something dark was also on the oil-cloth, covered by a grey fungus of delicate hairs.

Jane had asked him for his photograph, and he was bringing it. Ezekiel had had an idea that he was handsome. It was original with him, perhaps. But he had been told so by Jane and two or three others. His mother, to be sure, had once looked at him long and thoughtfully; "you will have to dress very well," she had said at last sadly. But though he was somewhat surprised at the time, he had come to think of it as a piece of transient melancholy. Now, as he thought of the picture of himself, he remembered the sadness in his mother's eyes as she had studied him. Somehow, he had not recognized himself at first; if he were older, it might have been as in the Japanese poem upon looking into a mirror: "Who is this old man whose face seems familiar?" He had seemed to himself an ordinary young man—another like himself in every car of the subway. But, as he had studied his own face, in time it had seemed not quite ordinary: in fact, he looked just like the swindlers whose pictures are printed in the papers—those who borrow money and promise three hundred per cent or sell stock for a simple invention to take the gold out of sea water. He wondered, but not anxiously, if Jane would see his photograph as he saw it.

She would be waiting for him, seated in front of the curtained window. It would be slightly open at the bottom, the wind blowing and troubling the curtain. Jane would be in her blue kimona, her feet in little blue slippers. These had an ornament in felt and gold thread. The design had probably been modeled on a leaf or a flower, but the copyist had obscured its meaning so that Ezekiel saw only patches of colored felt stitched with tinsel.

THE END

ABOUT THE AUTHOR

CHARLES REZNIKOFF, the son of Russian garment workers, was born in Brooklyn, New York, in 1894. He spent a year at the School of Journalism of the University of Missouri (1910–11) and was graduated from the Law School of New York University (LL.B., 1915). He was admitted to the bar of the State of New York in 1916 but never practiced law actively because he was primarily interested in writing. Between 1918 and 1961 he published twenty-three books of poetry and prose, including *By the Waters of Manhattan*, his first novel, in 1930. He began to gain a wider readership in 1962, when New Directions published a book of verse by the same title, *By the Waters of Manhattan: Selected Verse*. A second selection of poetry, *By the Well of Living and Seeing*, was published by Black Sparrow Press in 1974, followed by the *Complete Poems* (1976–77; revised 2005), edited by Seamus Cooney. The book-length poem, *Holocaust*, was Reznikoff's last major work. It was published in 1975, the year before his death at the age of eighty-one.

A NOTE ON THE TYPE

By the Waters of Manhattan has been set in Berthold type-foundry's Bodoni Old Face, a redrawing of the types designed by the distinguished printer Giambattista Bodoni (*1740–1813*). The son of a Piedmontese printer, Bodoni began his career as superintendent of the Press of the Propagation of the Faith in Rome. In 1786, he was named head of the ducal printing house in Parma, where he carried out his most important work as a typographer. Innovative in both type design and printing technique, Bodoni's books were widely admired for their meticulous presswork, opulent production, and generous formats—though his reputation as a printer of scholarly works was diminished by poor proofreading. ‡ While Bodoni's early work was executed under the influence of the Fourniers, the family of French typefounders and printers, it was the work of the English typographer John Baskerville that would most profoundly color his later output as a punchcutter and designer of books. The types Bodoni cut at the Stamperia Reale, considered the first "modern" faces, are widely admired for the pronounced contrast between thick and thin stroke, for their fine serifs, and for their openness and delicacy.

DESIGN AND COMPOSITION BY CARL W. SCARBROUGH